SECOND
CHOICE

DEBORAH WALLACE

Second Choice

Published by Deborah Wallace

Copyright © 2019 by Deborah Wallace

ISBN: 978-1-951457-00-6

Rev 2 6/25

Cover Art by Raymond and Deborah Wallace

Chapter 1

This time of morning was the best for running. Before work, Shannon Leonard had the park to herself most of the time. It woke her brain up better than coffee.

She got into a good rhythm and started through the day's patient list. First up was Mrs. O'Brien. The week before was her first visit. She'd had her cast removed from her wrist a couple weeks before and physical therapy exercises had been difficult for the elderly woman. The physical therapist had thought a few massage sessions before exercise might help.

Her next appointment was Jason Drexler, a beefy high school football player. He'd been a real handful the last three visits. It might be time to cut him, even though he said massage helped him with his game.

She entered the wooded area of the path, surprised to see a man stopped ahead with his head bent down. From the back, she could only guess that he was checking something on his phone. He wore a knit hat. Unusual, but not unheard of for an early June day.

A few steps away, she called out to him. "On your left."

She shifted to the opposite side of the narrow path, and held her arm close to her body, so she wouldn't brush against him. She came abreast of him, and he lunged out, grabbing both her arms from behind.

She yelped.

Her momentum almost toppled them, but he regained their balance. His left arm wrapped around her waist, trapping her arm. Something sharp pushed against her neck. She

1

was afraid if she breathed too hard, her throat would be cut. But she was already breathing hard from her run, and there was no way she could slow it down with her life threatened.

The steady rhythm of her heart from running was gone, replaced by an erratic beat that left her feeling weak. Any moment, her legs would give out. She didn't have anything of value on her. That meant he wanted to harm her. Rape! That kind of thing happened to other women, in fact, several in the past half year. She had enough bad things happen in her life, and couldn't take one more.

"Let me go, please. Please don't hurt me."

His hot breath rasped in her ear. "I've been watching you. We're going to have some fun."

She shivered. No, this wouldn't be fun. It had to be a nightmare, and she'd wake up any minute. Her nose filled with the scent of his aftershave as he pressed against her back. It was all too real. Stay calm. She could do this. The consequences were too scary to contemplate. Her self-defense refresher course had been six months ago, so she was as ready as she could ever be.

The voice of the trainer echoed through her head, giving her some much-needed courage. With her free hand, she grabbed his wrist and yanked it away, ducking under their arms. At this point, her training took over and she spun, and kicked as hard as she could into his groin. He groaned and stumbled to the ground. He wore a ski mask over his face.

Racing the fastest route home, she was afraid if she glanced over her shoulder, it would slow her down or she'd stumble, and he'd catch her again. She prayed that she wouldn't step on a hidden rock or trip over anything. With the house key in her hand, she paused only a second to open her door. Slamming and double locking it, she leaning over to catch her breath.

The police. She needed to call the police. Stumbling to

the couch, she collapsed. It took three tries to pull her phone from the holder on her upper arm. Her hands shook so much, that she kept hitting the wrong numbers as she dialed 911, grateful the number was short.

She couldn't hold back the sobs as she waited for someone to pick up. She had to calm down or they wouldn't understand her. Deep breath. Let it out. Deep breath.

"911. What's your emergency?"

She let her breath out and sucked in another. "Someone attacked me in the park with a knife."

"Do you need medical assistance?"

"No. I'm okay."

"Are you in a safe location?"

"Yes. I'm locked in my house." She scanned the room, not feeling totally safe, and hurried to the window, making sure it was locked.

"I'll send someone to speak with you."

"Thank you." She raced to each window and door in the house and checked the locks.

Back in the living room to await the police, adrenaline kept her in a frantic pace. She hoped someone arrived before she wore a hole in the floor.

She jumped at the knock on her front door, and peeked out the window. A dark car sat at the curb with the tell-tale antenna of an unmarked police vehicle. She relaxed a bit, and opened the door.

She sucked in a breath. A face from her nightmares. "No! No!" On top of the attack, she couldn't take seeing Luke. She tried to force the door closed.

He smashed his palm against the wood to keep it open, so she raced to the bathroom, needing to get there before he caught her. She slammed the door shut and locked it, putting her back to the cold surface, and crossed her arms.

His footsteps stopped with the thin barrier between them.

"I'm not talking to you, Luke. Go away." Panic had hit first, and then anger. The only person she wanted to see less than Luke was her attacker.

"Shannon, I'm the only one available to take your statement. You have to talk to me." His commanding voice made her angrier.

"No. Go away." She squeezed her eyes shut, swiping the tears off her cheeks. "I can't talk to you," she whispered, and clenched her hands over her stomach. She raised her voice. "I changed my mind. I don't want to report it."

She caught her face in the mirror over the sink, not sure if the pale skin was a result of the attack or Luke outside the door. A scratch on her neck reminded her of the blade against her throat. She swiped a shaky finger over it and checked it. Just a streak of blood. It could have been so much worse.

"Shannon, please," Luke said. "Your life might depend on it. And what about the other women he might attack?"

"Why you? I didn't even know you were back." She tried, but couldn't keep her voice from quivering. Couldn't she pretend he was a stranger? Her strong reaction took her by surprise, since she hadn't seen him in four years. If only she'd known, she could have prepared herself. Who was she kidding? There was no way she could have prepared for seeing the man who'd ripped out her heart when he told her he was marrying someone else. She took slow breaths, and tried to bury the pain he'd just dug up.

"I'm sorry you had to find out I'm back this way, but we need to talk about this guy who attacked you."

"Fine. Talk through the door." It sounded childish, but she couldn't be in the same room with him yet, and she could try to pretend he was someone else.

His exhale carried his frustration. "All right. We'll start this way. Where were you when he attacked?"

"I was running in the park."

4

"Oak Street Park?"

"Yes."

"Which part of the park?"

She shivered as she remembered the coolness of the shade and the sudden rough hands grabbing her arms. She stiffened her knees so she wouldn't slide down the door. "I'd just gotten onto the forest path."

"Where did he come from?"

"He was standing on the path, with his back to me. I assumed he was looking at his cell phone, but as I passed, he yanked me off my feet."

She felt dirty from the guy's hands on her, his body against her back. She forced the words out. "The guy said he'd been watching me, and we were going to have fun. Then he held a knife to my throat." She touched her neck. Her fear returned, although it hadn't totally left before. She'd almost been raped at knifepoint.

"Shannon, did he cut you?" That had to be fake panic in his voice.

Lifting her chin, she studied the mark on her neck again. "I've had worse scratches than this from briars."

His breath hissed out. "What happened after that?"

"I used some self-defense moves to break free then raced home in record time."

"I need to see your neck. I need to see if he left any other marks on you. And then we should take you to the hospital."

"Luke, no." She couldn't let him touch her. His touch would bring back torturous memories she'd buried long ago.

"It's important. This may be The Slasher."

She gasped and her heart jumped into her throat. "The man who killed three women?" And raped them. Thank God for the instinct that told her the man planned to rape her, and that she hadn't thought about murder, or she might have panicked into a stupor. She'd barely escaped death.

Shannon unlocked the door and opened it. She stood in front of Luke, dazed, and peeked up at him. The corners of his dark brown eyes had crinkles they didn't have before. He looked older than her brother, who was the same age. His hair still had curls, ones she used to love running her fingers through. She shut that thought down. His shoulders were broader than she remembered, and maybe he was an inch or two taller. He wore a short-sleeved button-down shirt and blue jeans. If she didn't hate him so much, she'd find him attractive.

"I was almost kidnapped by The Slasher?" She grabbed the jamb as trembles weakened her body. She could have been brutally murdered like the other women.

Luke grasped her hand and wrapped his arm around her. She wanted to pull away, but was afraid she'd crumple to the floor without his support.

"Come on. I still have a few more questions." His gentle voice was a balm covering the fear that'd raced through her since the man attacked her. She didn't want him to affect her in any way. He led her to the living room and turned on a light. "Let me see your neck." He lifted up her chin, and sucked in a breath.

"I think he's right-handed. Hold on while I get a picture." He pulled out his cell phone and clicked a few shots. "Do you have any other injuries?"

"I'll probably have bruises on my upper arms from where he grabbed me, and my ribs hurt from his arm around me." She pulled up her shirt to show him. At Luke's indrawn breath she glanced at her ribs and up at him. "What? There's nothing there."

"Nothing, but perfection." Luke smiled, and she yanked her shirt back down.

Yeah, engage brain now. She should have just said she was fine.

His expression changed to serious again. "So, you probably don't need to see a doctor. The cut on your neck is just a scratch, and your ribs seem fine." He touched above a red mark on her upper arm. "This might become a bruise where he grabbed you."

She hadn't noticed the mark. She glanced at her other arm, which was unmarred.

"Now, can you tell me anything about how big he was, and how he looked or moved?"

Shannon shook her head. She stared at her twisting hands so that she wouldn't have to see his face, not that it helped her to forget who she was talking to. Just hearing that voice over the phone would melt her. But not now. "Not really. I didn't pay attention when I thought he was on his phone. He just seemed average. When I broke free, I saw he was wearing a ski mask. Um, he wasn't overweight."

"All right, I'm going to stand behind you to help you get a sense of his size."

She nodded warily.

Luke put his left arm around her waist and the right arm up with his hand beside her throat. She stiffened, not wanting him touching her. In one way, it was worse than the man in the park. The part of her heart that she'd walled off and let freeze was screaming in pain. The only consolation was that the worst of the panic from the park had passed.

"Relax, Shannon."

Relax? Between the reminder that a rapist/killer had held her like this, and Luke even touching her, she couldn't relax. For the longest time, she'd wanted him to come back to her, tell her it had all been a terrible mistake, and wrap his arms around her. That time was gone. The only way she'd found to deal with it was to hate him.

"Is this how he held you?"

She closed her eyes and tried not to think about this being Luke, how he smelled like she remembered, how he warmed her as they snuggled and watched TV. She nodded, and concentrated on the killer's arms and hands on her. It was an overload to her emotions—fear, hurt, anger, and longing.

"Think about size. Is this the angle he held the knife?" There was a slight pressure on her throat, probably a finger.

"I think it was lower. His arm was against my shoulder and his voice was closer to my ear. He must have been shorter."

"Good. Did he have his body right up against you?" Luke demonstrated and Shannon tried even harder not to notice that it was Luke's warm body behind her. "Could you tell if he was thin or muscular?"

"He was average." Shannon grabbed the arm at her throat and swung under so that she stood beside him then quickly released his arm. She took a step back and drew in a long breath, trying to regain her sanity. "His arm muscles were hard, but he wasn't muscular like a body builder." Her gaze dropped to Luke's arms. They were bigger than she remembered, too. Another thought to bury.

"Nice move. Good. Do you always run at the same time?"

"Yes, six-thirty, Tuesday, Thursday and Saturday."

"He knew you'd be there this morning. You should stop running for a while or run with other people."

"I like the quiet of early morning, and I've got to get it done before work."

He glared his disapproval.

"Okay. I won't run in the woods. I'll stay in the open areas of the park."

"Shannon, it's not safe until we catch him."

She lifted her chin. "I took care of myself this morning." She'd be more careful. She had pepper spray in her purse.

She'd carry it, ready to use when she ran. She was being a bit foolish, but she didn't want to take orders from Luke.

"Yeah, but now he knows what you can do, and he'll be more prepared next time."

"You think he'll try again?" Her emotions were a roller coaster, the excitement of the climb and the terror of the descent—over and over. She couldn't identify the man. Wouldn't he think of her as too much of a challenge and go after an easier target? Not that she wanted another woman to be raped and murdered.

"I wouldn't bet against it." He strode to the door and turned back. "Lock this." He scanned the room. "Lock all your doors and windows."

And then he was gone, leaving her shaken. She collapsed on the floor, feeling like she'd been attacked twice.

~~~

Thursday morning, Shannon opened her front door to find Luke waiting on her doorstep in running clothes. He looked good in his tank top, shorts, and tan. He always did tan faster than her. His legs were more muscled than she remembered.

Closing her eyes, she took a deep breath, trying to fortify her walls and pretend Luke was just any other guy. She'd keep her gaze and thoughts on running—one foot in front of the other and ignore him. Once she got rid of him.

She barely glanced at his face and stared into the street. "What are you doing here?"

"I didn't expect you to take my advice, so I'm running with you."

"I should have expected you to show up. And no, you're not." She lifted her hand, showing him her pepper spray. "I've got extra protection."

He lifted his brows. "You think *that* would protect you from a determined killer?"

She glared at him.

"Fine. I'll stay behind you. You won't even know I'm here."

If he got something in his head that he was going to do, nothing could stop him. Like when Luke thought the eight-year-old girl who lived next door to her parents was being abused by the mother's boyfriend. He talked to the mother. She wouldn't believe him. He skulked around the house, ready to take pictures through windows. One day, something in the other house crashed and the girl cried. Luke raced to a window, snapped a couple pictures, then ran to the back door, throwing it open with a bang. He attacked the man and called the police. His pictures showed the man's arm raised over the girl, with a broom in his hand. She had a broken arm, but it could have been so much worse.

That was the kind of guy he'd always been—protecting those who needed help. It'd been his reason for joining the police force. In the end, he hadn't wanted to protect her.

She ignored him, grabbed the railing for balance and lifted and lowered each knee a few times.

"Shannon, I—"

She shook a finger at him. "You don't get to talk." For the next stretch, she kicked out her foot. She tried her hardest to ignore Luke's eyes on her. She wondered if he'd already stretched. No. She didn't care. She did a few lunges with one foot forward, then the other and finished by kicking each foot high behind her, then started her run.

Today, Shannon was too frazzled to organize her day. She'd have to review her patients' treatment plans once she got to the office. She had to keep dragging her mind back to work because she didn't want to think about Luke. Behind her, his footfalls and breathing were an unwelcome distraction.

If she really needed a bodyguard, she wished he would assign someone else to run with her. But that wouldn't suit his purpose.

She'd called her brother after seeing Luke two days before. He'd known that Luke had been back for a couple of weeks. *Nice of Will to not tell me.* Maybe she should be the one to consider leaving town this time. But she had her family and friends here. She wouldn't let him drive her away from them. If only he'd leave her alone, then she could pretend again that he didn't exist.

She liked her town. Big enough that there was always something to do, but not so big that everybody was a stranger. And the traffic wasn't so bad.

She'd heard that Annie died, the woman Luke had left her for. A surge of satisfaction welled up that he'd been left alone, but she ignored it. She wouldn't have wished the woman dead. It was Luke's choice that she hated. She hadn't expected him to return to town, and wished he'd stayed away. He had to know how much he'd hurt her.

She kicked up her speed, her breath rasping in and out, and wished she could leave the pain behind as easily as she left Luke trailing in her dust.

Shannon finished her run in near record time and raced up her steps. Quickly unlocking her door, she slammed it shut and locked it before Luke had even crossed the street.

If only she could lock him out of her thoughts as easily.

~~~

Luke would have preferred running beside Shannon and trying to get her to talk to him, but he had a great view from behind. Her narrow waist flared into that tight butt that his hands itched to hold as he pumped into her. Her auburn ponytail swayed with each step. Sunlight turned it to a burnished red. He wondered if it was as soft as he remembered.

Her golden-brown eyes used to be full of fun and laughter, but now they glared at him with hatred or pain. He'd done that to her. Her face was thinner, too. When he'd left, she'd looked younger than her twenty-two years. Now, at twenty-six, she looked closer to her age, and still beautiful.

They passed the fenced in playground, and he scanned it and the street beyond. No kids, no runners. His senses went on high alert as they headed into the small wooded area.

With his two previous successes at identifying serial killers, he'd been asked to head up the serial killer taskforce in his old home town. He'd planned to come back all along, but it was harder than he expected. His best friend wouldn't speak to him. Not surprising since Shannon was Will's sister. Some of his other friends had abandoned him, too.

He'd wanted Shannon to get used to seeing him around town before approaching her. That got ripped from his hands when she'd been attacked, and he had to talk to her. He'd almost lost her before seeing her again. He would have given anything for her not to have been targeted, even giving up this excuse to be near her.

He wanted to hold her in his arms and never let go, but he had to get her to talk to him first and hopefully, convince her to forgive him. At this point, he didn't see it happening, but he wasn't giving up. And even if she never talked to him, he wouldn't abandon her to a killer.

He still hadn't come up with a way to apologize to her. How could a guy apologize for leaving his girlfriend, his everything, to marry another woman? He'd known it was a mistake moments after the ceremony in front of the judge. Too many times, he berated himself for rushing to fix one problem without taking the time to think it all through. Of course, given a clearer head, he'd thought of better alternatives later.

When it was too late.

He picked up speed, but she did, too, keeping him behind her. He'd give her the time she needed to get used to him, but he wouldn't disappear this time.

He'd thought that when he saw her again, he'd feel affection for her, but he'd been taken by surprise by how the love welled up, and burst through his heart, making it ache. As time went on, it had gotten easier to not think of her, but the best part of himself had been missing. When he'd put his arm around her to demonstrate the killer's hold, it had taken everything he had to not hug her tighter and kiss her neck. For just a moment, his heart felt whole.

They rounded the open fields. On weekends, they'd be filled with soccer games and cheering families. Weekdays, after school, boys threw footballs. One last sprint past houses and across the street, they reached Shannon's house.

With one foot on the bottom step, Luke gasped for breath. He definitely needed to run more. The first part had been fine, but Shannon increased her pace just as he would have normally finished his own run, and he had a hard time keeping up.

Shannon lived in a ranch style duplex with no garages. Two cars sat in the neighbor's double-wide driveway. A similar building sat on each side of hers.

After a few more minutes of staring at Shannon's door, he walked back to his car. He had a killer to catch.

Chapter 2

Saturday morning, Shannon stepped out of her door fifteen minutes earlier than usual and found Luke waiting for her. She'd hoped to be well on her way by the time he showed up. He knew her better than she thought he did. "Oh, you're here."

Luke smiled. "Shannon, if you don't want to run with me, find another run buddy or run at the school track. There are at least ten people there in the morning."

"I don't like the track. I like running in the park and woods." About half the path she ran wended through heavy trees but still had a wide, smooth surface. The rest had grass, flowers and a few trees. She warmed up and started running.

Once they hit the woods, Luke sped up beside Shannon. Before she could speed away, he spoke. "We found another one."

She didn't glance at him, considered ignoring his statement, but curiosity grabbed her. "Another what?"

"Body. This morning."

She stopped so fast Luke shot past her and had to come back.

After the attack, she'd read everything she could find on The Slasher. He killed about once a month. Two days short of a month she'd been attacked. Of course, he wouldn't have been satisfied when he'd lost her.

"Oh, my God. She died because he didn't get me." That could have been her if she hadn't fought back and taken him by surprise. She hated that this other woman had taken her place.

"It's not your fault."

She stared at her hands, interlacing her fingers, weaving and reweaving them. Another woman's life had been snuffed out. "But I couldn't help you catch him."

"We know more than we did before. We'll get him, but this is even more reason for you to be careful." He reached out as if to take her arm, but dropped his hand.

Hearing about the other woman's death, just days after the attack on her, increased the fear of what she'd escaped. All the women had been raped before they were murdered. And maybe the news reports didn't release all the information. Their last hours could have been even more brutal.

"All right, fine. I won't leave for my run before you get here. But I wish you'd assign someone else to run with me."

"Not happening, Shannon. And when you leave for work, look out the window to make sure there's no one suspicious around. And when you leave work, go with a group or have someone walk you out."

After killing someone else, she would have thought the killer had moved on, but Luke thought she was still in danger. "All right, I will." Instead of trembling at the reminder of her close call, she poured that energy into running again, concentrating on her pace so that she wouldn't have to think about anything else.

~~~

Luke kept pace beside her and was surprised that Shannon didn't increase her speed to get ahead of him. She'd been rattled when he told her about the latest victim. Maybe she felt safer with him at her side. He hoped so. It was a start, trusting him with her life. Now, he had to figure out how to get her to trust him with her heart again.

If the killer stayed true to form, there wouldn't be another death for at least a month, keeping Shannon safe. He hoped the killer wouldn't hunt her, but he'd take no chances, at least keeping her safe on her runs. He hoped she took the threat seriously when he wasn't with her.

He didn't run with his gun, not wanting it on full display. In the case of this killer, he could handle himself just fine against a knife. Throughout the run, he kept a vigilant eye out for anyone or anything out of place.

Two blocks from Shannon's house, she sped up. This time he crossed the street before she slammed her door.

He gripped the porch railing as he caught his breath. Shannon wasn't ready to listen to him yet. He'd known he'd hurt her, but hadn't realized how deeply. Her overreaction at seeing him had taken him by surprise, but it shouldn't have. He'd tried a few times shortly after he left to call her, but she wouldn't pick up. She probably didn't listen to his voicemail either. He hoped the anger meant she still had some love for him. To have any chance, he needed a way to break through the pain he'd caused. Then maybe he could start healing the hurt.

He'd take it slow, giving her time to see he still loved her, that he hadn't stopped. Being with her these brief times, and seeing the pain he'd inflicted, made his heart ache and regret even more the choices he'd made.

~~~

Luke walked through the office area, the detective's desks all in a line. Half were currently occupied, the rest held personal items and folders, showing the owners would return. He detoured to the desk of his assistant in the serial killer case. He'd only worked with Gary Wassman for a few weeks, but he was proving to be a perceptive detective.

"Hey, Gary. Did you find out anything more about this

morning's victim?"

"Yeah. Jordan Ford. She was only nineteen. She visited her aunt in New York for a week. All the danger she could have run into in New York City, and she came home to this," he said with disgust.

"Anything else?"

"She arrived on the six-twenty-five bus. Her apartment is only three blocks from the depot, so she walked. A couple of people saw her get off the bus with a wheeled suitcase. So, he abducted her somewhere between the bus stop and home. Her parents reported her missing about midnight. She was supposed to have dinner with them. They called all her friends in hopes that she'd gone somewhere else."

"Anyone see her after she left the station?"

"We haven't found anyone yet."

"Okay, thanks." Luke took a step away and turned back. "What about her suitcase?"

"It hasn't turned up."

Luke went into his office and sat at his desk. He picked up the closest stack of papers. The previous day, he handed one of the officers a list of questions and asked him to compile it on each victim. He was happy to note that it was organized neatly and even had a comments section for additional information. At the top of the page was a picture. Under that was age and occupation, followed by address and who they lived with. It continued to list the date and day of the week they disappeared and location, where and how they were found and how they died. He set the pages side by side in order.

Luke studied the pictures first. He noticed that all the victims had a shade of red hair. The first one was a bright, unnatural red. The second had auburn hair a little darker than Shannon's. The third was a strawberry blonde. The one found that morning had orange-red hair. Five redheaded

17

women couldn't be a coincidence.

He'd have Gary send a bulletin to the news outlets warning that the killer was targeting women with red hair. Maybe some women would temporarily dye their hair. He wondered if it was too late for Shannon to change her hair color since she'd already been chosen. Protected by hair color. He rubbed a hand down his face. Hair color was a crazy feature to be drawn to, but serial killers weren't known to be sane, average people.

The two previous serial killer cases he'd worked weren't as tough as this one. It was a lot harder when the woman he loved was a target. He had trouble concentrating when thoughts of Shannon's safety were never far from his mind. He needed to protect her, even though she didn't want him around and wouldn't follow his suggestions on how to keep safe.

People never expect to be the target—apparently, even ones who've already been targeted.

He dragged his mind back to the victims. They deserved his full attention to find their killer.

Two of the women had been snatched on a Wednesday and two on a Friday. Either it didn't have significance or it made Shannon an aberration. She'd been attacked on Tuesday. It was very early in the morning. Maybe this guy tried to kidnap her before going to work. Were the others kidnapped on days he didn't work late or didn't have other things to do?

The third victim, Mary Roth, had been abducted on a Friday at the park across from the school where she taught. On nice days, she was seen correcting papers or reading in the park between three-thirty and five o'clock. She lived alone in a third-floor apartment.

Luke studied the other victims. The first victim was an unidentified hitchhiker. She was last seen at a diner on a Wednesday. Her body had been found on the entrance ramp to the highway. One of the waitresses at the diner said the girl had been on her way to stay with a friend in New Jersey.

The previous detective had the New Jersey state police put her picture on the air. Over three months and they still didn't have a name. Did her family wonder where she was? Maybe he should send bulletins to all the surrounding states.

What was the significance of red hair to the killer? Did he know one of the women and the other killings covered up the association? Maybe he was angry at a redhead he couldn't take his anger out on. There were too many questions and no answers.

Luke ran his hand over his face again and stared at the pages. None of the women were married. They all lived alone, and only one had an on again off again boyfriend— Jordan Ford. He'd bet that they were currently not dating. Did this guy select women who lived alone so that no one would notice they were missing until after their bodies were found? Did he follow them, get to know their routines? Or was it just chance that all the women lived alone?

Luke leaned back in his chair. The killer was careful. At this point, the only way to get more information would be to find another dead woman. He didn't want more deaths to pile up. Most of these women had people whose lives were destroyed by their loss. That didn't even take into consideration the suffering these women experienced before they were murdered.

Chapter 3

Every Tuesday, Thursday and Saturday morning for over two weeks, Luke showed up at Shannon's house to run with her. He kept pace better now, but Shannon suspected that he occasionally tested the waters to see if she'd let him near her. It was probably childish, but it was better for her heart to ignore him. The less she saw of him, the less she heard his voice, the easier it was to not think of him.

This Saturday, Shannon worked on distractions, thinking of anything but him. Work, her grocery list, what movie she wanted to see with her friends, her niece and nephew. Anything, but the man behind her. His voice caught her by surprise.

"Shannon, we need to talk."

"No." Even that one word meant she was encouraging him to say more.

"I still love you."

"You don't know what that means. You said the same words the day you left me." She sped up and Luke fell behind again. He couldn't think that telling her would make her melt. It wouldn't work on her anymore. He couldn't be trusted. She wouldn't be second choice.

Shannon raced like the devil was chasing her and slammed her front door between them, locked it and leaned against it. *Why did he have to come back? She'd been doing fine, hadn't she?* She had friends she enjoyed spending time with. She could have a good time. Brenda and Beth were going to a movie with her that afternoon and then they'd have dinner. They'd have a wonderful time.

She wasn't depressed anymore. At least she hadn't been until a few weeks ago.

~~~

Luke parked beside his mother's car in front of his apartment and headed inside. His living room held comfortable furniture that was a reminder of the home he used to have, and followed the voices coming from the kitchen.

"Daddy!" The little girl jumped out of her chair. Luke squatted down to let his five-year-old daughter run into his arms. He stood and ran his fingers through her soft, dark curls.

"Hi, Sherry. Have you been good for Grandma?"

"Yes, Daddy. Grandma is fun."

He couldn't have done this move without his mother. She'd found this apartment for him and daycare for Sherry. She took care of Sherry whenever he needed to work outside of school or daycare hours. She'd only seen Sherry a handful of times before he moved back home. Now, day by day, love blossomed between them.

If only he could have that effect on a certain redhead. Keeping her safe was only a start.

"Thanks for coming out again, Mom. I hate to have you get up so early."

"That's all right. It's for a good cause." Elaine patted his arm.

Luke kissed his daughter's forehead. "Hey, sprite, why don't you go get dressed, and then we'll go to the playground, and after that, we'll do something special." He set her on her feet, and she scampered off.

He sat in the chair his daughter had vacated and rubbed his temples.

"It looks like it's not going well," Elaine said.

"No, she won't let me talk to her. Anytime I try, she just runs off."

"That's what you did to her. I can't say I blame her."

His heart twisted. "Mom—"

"Luke, I know your situation. I know why you left, but I was here and watched Shannon fall apart."

He dropped his head, his heart aching. "You didn't tell me."

She squeezed his hand. "You chose your path. Telling you would have made it more difficult for you."

Now that he was back, he wasn't sure how he'd been able to leave Shannon. He'd been a stupid kid at twenty-three. Not really a kid, but definitely stupid.

He was beginning to feel that there was nothing he could do to change Shannon's mind. How could he when she wouldn't talk to him? Words of love hadn't worked anyway. He needed actions that would prove his love. It was a vicious, interconnected circle.

"It'll be hard for her to forgive you."

"Thanks for the encouragement, Mom." But she was right. He'd been oblivious to how he'd hurt Shannon, stuck in his own little world. He thought he was making a difference, and he had, but hadn't realized the sacrifices he'd forced on Shannon.

Elaine shrugged and patted his hand.

"Today I told her I loved her, and she said that's what I said the day I left." Of course it would have sounded like a lie. A man who loved a woman wouldn't leave her.

"Maybe you need some actions that show how much you love her."

"I need Shannon to understand about Annie before we can move forward together." If they ever got together. He ran a hand down his face. "How do I get her to listen to me?"

"Honey, maybe you have to listen to her first."

He stared at her. "And how do I do that?"

She gave him an impish grin. "Maybe you have to run faster than she does." She stood and dropped her hand to his shoulder. "I'll see you Tuesday."

He covered her hand and squeezed. "Thanks again, Mom."

He'd been dropping his daughter at daycare each week-day morning and then the school bus would pick her up there to take her to kindergarten. Since he'd been running with— *Yeah, right*, behind—Shannon, his mom had come over to take care of Sherry since it was too early for daycare.

As she left, Luke headed for the shower. He ran his hands through his hair. Over the past four years, he'd been able to wall up thoughts of Shannon most of the time, but a piece of his heart had always hurt. For both of them.

It was good to be back in his hometown. He just had to mend some fences. He hoped to run into Shannon's brother at the playground. He'd seen Will there a couple of times with his two children. They'd been best friends since fourth grade, until he'd walked out on Shannon. Twice, when Luke saw him in town, Will had fled into the first available door when Luke started towards him. He smiled and wondered if Will had gotten Leah any sexy lingerie when he'd stepped into that erotic clothing store.

Freshly showered, Luke stopped at his daughter's bed-room. "Ready to go, sprite?"

Sherry dropped the large puzzle piece onto the half-finished puzzle on the floor, and scrambled up. "Yes!" She raced past him to the door, sat and slipped on her shoes.

He took her hand and went out the door. Since Simon's Tot Park was two blocks from Luke's apartment, they walked. He hoped Sherry would be tired out enough that he'd get to carry her on the way home. She was a major reason for leaving Shannon, and he needed that connection to his past.

Sherry had only recently started to heal from losing her mother. It had been a few weeks since she'd asked if her mother would be able to find them in their new home. There was a fine balance between keeping memories of Annie alive and helping Sherry deal with the loss. He wasn't always successful. He missed her, too, which made it doubly difficult.

A half block from the park, Sherry tugged at his hand. "Hurry, Daddy."

Luke smiled. "The park's not going anywhere, sprite. We still have to cross the street."

Sherry stopped beside him at the crosswalk and only started forward when he did. "Daddy, I see Willa. Let's hurry." She started tugging again.

"Willa?" He studied her. Will's daughter?

She glanced up, and then back to the other girl. "She's my friend. She sits at my table and we play together when we go outside for recess."

He smiled. His daughter didn't have it easy. A few months after her mother died, he uprooted her to move here. He was glad she'd made a friend. He just hoped Will wouldn't snatch that friendship away.

Once they'd crossed the street, Luke pointed to a park bench at the edge of the playground where another man spread out, one arm on the armrest and the other draped across the back, his legs stretched in front of him. "I'm going to sit on the dad bench."

He let go of her hand, and she raced toward her friend. He came up behind the bench and froze. Will. He should have recognized that sprawl.

He should find a different bench, but he'd already told Sherry where he'd be. Luke circled around to the front, and sat. Will scowled at him, stood, and opened his mouth to call out to his children.

"Please don't," he said.

Will glanced at him, then faced the playground.

"Willa is Sherry's first friend here."

The two children looked so happy playing together. He'd hate to have Willa leave as soon as she got there. Finally, Will sat back down.

"Thank you."

Will's mouth hardened. At least he wasn't taking his anger at Luke out on their daughters.

This might be the only chance Luke had to start to mend his friendship with Will. Kind of hard to hang up when you're sitting next to the person. "If I could do it over again, I wouldn't have left Shannon. It was the biggest mistake I ever made." He glanced at Will's frozen face and away again.

It took Luke by surprise when Will responded a few moments later. "What? It didn't work out with your wife, so you're back to destroy Shannon's life again?"

Pain sliced through Luke's heart. Maybe Will hadn't heard that Annie died. He couldn't be that callus.

Annie had been a childhood friend, almost like a sister. She'd lived in the next town with her parents, friends of his parents. Through the years, they visited often, back-and-forth. Will had known of her, but they'd never met.

Luke's marriage to Annie had been based on their love for Sherry, and his concern for Annie's health. If he'd been able to return to Shannon sooner, then Annie's life would have been shorter. He had mixed feelings about it, and guilt. At times, thoughts of Shannon had popped into his head, and he'd wish his time away from her were over.

Luke buried the grief. "I don't ever want to hurt Shannon again."

The pain in Will's eyes was echoed in his voice. "Then leave her alone. She nearly didn't survive the first time you abandoned her." He got up and stalked away.

Luke sat, stunned. What did he mean by that? Did she try to commit suicide? Would he send her into depression if he continued his pursuit? Luke covered his eyes, then ran his hand down his face. He'd known it would be hard to get Shannon to trust him again, but he hadn't realized how huge the obstacles would be.

Sherry and Willa giggled as they ran, hand-in-hand, to the swings, breaking apart to flop on their bellies in the seats, pushing themselves high in the air. Their friendship so much like the one their fathers used to have.

Chapter 4

Officer Adam Williams called Luke after dinner to tell him of an abducted police woman. After he dropped Sherry at his mother's house, he headed to the crime scene. One of their own this time. It may have been unrelated to the serial killer case, a criminal trying to get back at the officer. But his gut told him this was another one.

The timing was right.

The killer likely wanted them to know that not even a trained police officer was safe, taunting them with their incompetence.

He parked behind a police cruiser, scanning the middle-class neighborhood as he climbed out. Small side yards and driveways separated most houses. Some had garages. The houses sat fairly close together and most yards appeared well groomed. It'd been dark for an hour or so, but the street lights illuminated the area well.

Despite the police car, no neighbors had come out to investigate.

He approached the uniformed officer standing at the door of a house across the street from his cruiser. "Hi, Adam. Thanks for calling me in. Which officer is it?"

Adam spoke in a low voice. "Jane Roslin. I called the captain, too, so he could personally tell the others. I couldn't say anything over the radio. Everybody likes Jane, so I didn't want it to get out like that." Adam was a bit pale and flustered, not the usual, efficient officer. He pointed to the house across the street. "Over there is where Jane lives."

Luke nodded. He remembered meeting Jane when introductions were made at the police station. She'd been one of the few faces who hadn't been there when he left. She was friendly and open, and offered her assistance in capturing the killer. He recalled her auburn hair and now was nearly one-hundred-percent sure she was another victim of the serial killer. They'd probably have a better chance of rescuing her if the abduction was related to one of her cases.

Adam touched the door in front of him. The house directly across from Jane's. The man's hand shook as he stuck his thumb through a belt loop. "I was just talking with this neighbor when you drove up. She saw Jane's abduction about an hour ago."

"All right," Luke said grimly. "Let's talk to this neighbor." It had been four weeks since the last murder.

He followed Adam into the house. They stopped in front of a gray-haired woman seated in an upholstered chair in the living room. Her bright blue eyes probably missed nothing. "Ms. Somers, this is Detective Luke Cade. Luke, this is Meredith Somers."

She glanced between them. "Have a seat." Her bony fingers pointed to the couch. "And please call me Meredith."

Luke sat at the edge of the cushion, close to her. "Meredith, Officer Williams told me that you saw someone take Jane."

She nodded and twisted her hands together. "I was about to go meet friends. Since the...murders have started, I always peek out the window before I open the door. This time I saw a dark colored car across the street. A man got out when Jane pulled into her driveway."

"Can you tell me what he looked like?"

She shook her head. "He had a hood pulled up, so I couldn't see his face."

"Was he tall or short? Thin or heavy?"

Meredith rubbed her fingers over her lips. "He wasn't heavy, but not thin either. I don't know about height."

"Was he taller than Jane when he grabbed her?"

She closed her eyes. "He was…just a little taller than Jane."

"Good. What did he do after he got out of his car?"

"Jane hadn't noticed him and started to walk toward her house. He ran up and grabbed her from behind. She struggled and kicked and then she went limp."

Luke leaned forward. "What did he do then?"

"He dragged her to his car, and shoved her into the backseat. Then he leaned in for a few seconds. After that, he ran around to the driver's side, and drove off."

Luke nodded. "Did you happen to get a license plate number?"

Meredith shook her head. "I didn't think about it right away. I only saw the first number, seven. And it was a state plate."

"Do you know what kind of car?"

"I'm not very much into cars. Sorry."

They were lucky she'd seen anything, but he'd known she likely wouldn't recognize the kind of car. "It was a four-door. How big was it?" Luke asked.

She pursed her lips. "It was bigger than my car. Do you mind if I check the other ones outside?"

"Sure. Let's go." Meredith energetically sprung from her chair, and Luke led the way to the front steps.

Two more police cars were parked on this side of the street. Three officers ran flashlights over the ground in front of Jane's house.

She scanned the street. "It's not as big as your cars. It's about the size of that one." She pointed to her neighbor's car.

"Can you be more specific than dark colored?"

She shook her head. "I'm sorry. It could have been

black, dark blue, dark gray." She waved toward the light at the corner. "These street lights tend to make colors look like mud."

"Thanks for your help, Meredith. Here's my card. If you think of anything else, give me a call."

She tightened her fingers around the card until it curled. "I wish I could help you more."

Luke patted her upper arm. "The most important thing is that you saw what happened to Jane and reported it right away. We might not have known for a while." Not until Jane's body turned up. "Your description of the car helps, too."

Luke and Adam crossed to Jane's driveway. The fact that Jane had slumped after struggling with her attacker, led him to believe that she'd been drugged. The man would have studied her, and known that a police officer could hold her own in a fair fight.

Adam shook his head. "I don't envy you your job. Too much pressure to get the killer before he takes another life."

"Yeah, that's the hard part. On my last case, there were ten deaths that we know of before we caught the guy." He nodded toward the other officers. "I'm going to see if they've found anything. Are you coming?"

Adam stared at the activity, then glanced at him. "Do you mind if I don't?" His hands opened and closed at his sides. Maybe Jane hadn't been just another officer to Adam.

"No, it's fine. See you later, Adam."

Luke retrieved a flashlight from his car and joined the officers to see what they'd found.

He stopped at the closest man. They hadn't talked much since Luke got back. "Hi, Juan. Find anything?"

Juan lifted a plastic bag. "Keys. They belong to Jane."

Luke studied the house, finding a camera on the eave pointing toward the driveway. "Has anybody been inside

30

yet?"

"No."

Luke held out his hand. "Can I have the keys?" He took the bag, and rushed to the front door. He punched the point of the key through the bag, being careful not to disturb possible fingerprints on the key head. He opened the door, and flipped on the lights, revealing a comfortable living room. A wide screen TV sat on a stand with books on shelves under it. A tan couch with matching pillows faced it. He hoped she'd come back to this, that she'd find a way to escape.

The security panel was near the door. He didn't know how to operate it, but he called the company number written on the panel, introduced himself and requested a copy of the footage be sent to the police station.

~~~

The next morning, Shannon wasn't surprised that Luke waited on her doorstep. She stepped out, having already done her warm-ups inside, and started her run.

He fell in beside her. "I got a call last night about a police woman being kidnapped."

She glanced at him, but quickly returned her gaze to the path.

"She struggled, but he must have knocked her out somehow. He learned from you that kidnapping at knife point isn't always successful."

She was sure he meant that she wouldn't stand a chance if the man tried again to kidnap her. She wanted to forget it ever happened, but it wouldn't keep her safe.

Luke smacked his fist into his palm. "Jane would have whipped his butt if it had been a knife."

Shannon froze, and her heart rate kicked up faster than it already had been. It couldn't be. "Jane Roslin?"

Luke stopped beside her and frowned. "Yeah, do you know her?"

Not Jane! Jane was one of the kindest people Shannon knew. She was always trying to help people. She'd helped Shannon and so many other women.

"We worked together as waitresses at the *Oakland Diner* when we were in college. Then Jane decided to go to the police academy. I haven't seen her in about six months." Shannon was still warm from running, but a chill overtook it. She rubbed her hands on her arms. Shannon stared at Luke. "Do you think you'll find her before he kills her?"

"I hope so, but we didn't get enough information from the witness. At least this time we had a witness." Luke massaged the back of his neck. "We're a long way from solving this."

His news brought the killings closer to home. A friend had been kidnapped, and if she wasn't found quickly, she'd die like the other women.

Shannon started running again, and thoughts jumbled through her head. She'd enjoyed working with Jane. They used to point out cute guys to each other and make up stories about them. Sometimes they started giggling and the diner owner would glare at them, which stopped it pretty quickly. It wasn't the same at the diner after Jane left. She used to come back in for meals during her police training and they'd talk. Jane was the reason Shannon had taken self-defense courses.

She might never see her friend again. Shannon wished she'd kept in touch. In some convoluted way it felt like, if they'd remained close, this wouldn't have happened to Jane.

Shannon stopped running again as another realization dawned on her. "Jane saved my life."

Luke stopped beside her and lifted one eyebrow. "What do you mean?"

She tried to slow down her breathing, but the more her guilt took hold, the harder it was. Her eyes flooded. She blinked rapidly, but one tear streaked down her cheek, and she swiped it away. "Jane talked me into taking the self-defense course she was helping teach. I refused twice before she got me to agree. It was fun, and I've taken refresher courses." She blinked back more tears. "I got away because of her, but she couldn't get away because of me."

Luke put his hands on her arms and held firmly. "Shannon, you know Jane would be happy to know that she helped keep you alive. Besides, the killer would have known she was a trained police officer. You also know she's not going to give up trying to escape."

Shannon nodded and took a trembling breath. Jane had to find a way to escape. She took another, steadier breath and stepped back from Luke. His hands dropped to his sides as his gaze stayed on her. She ran. If she didn't, she'd probably curl up in a ball and cry like a baby.

She didn't know anyone as determined as Jane. Her friend would keep trying. Shannon had to believe that.

~~~

After Shannon raced into her house, Luke returned to the park. The week before, he'd continued running after leaving Shannon. He ran the same loop that they covered together. Sort of. So far, he'd tired before completing it. He came out of the woods, pushing to go a little farther than the previous time. This was the third extra session, and he'd made progress before he had to slow down.

He cut through the middle of the park, still keeping a close eye out for anyone hiding behind a tree, or trying to appear harmless on a park bench, while watching for another unsuspecting woman. Although, they likely had a month before it happened again.

A half block left, his breathing close to normal, he sprinted. His goal was to do the whole loop again after Shannon finished. Then he'd be on her heals as she reached her door, and he'd give her no choice, except to let him into her house. Then they'd have the talk she'd been denying him.

Chapter 5

Breakfast with his mother was always better than when he had to throw it together. Sherry ended up with cold cereal, and he usually had a bagel. Luke patted his stomach. Nothing could top her pancakes and bacon.

He checked in his rearview mirror. Sherry sat in her car seat with her arms crossed on her small chest.

"Hey, sprite, what's with the long face?"

She made a dramatic sigh. "I 'membered Willa has a doctor 'pointment today."

It might be a long, lonely day for his daughter. "Maybe you should try to make a new friend today. Then tomorrow, you'll have two friends to play with. You can introduce her to Willa."

"I don't know how. Willa made friends with me."

Luke pulled into the daycare parking lot and got out. He opened the back door and sat down as he unbuckled Sherry, then sat her on his lap. "Why don't you find someone who's alone and looks sad? Go up to her and say, 'Hi. My name's Sherry. Do you want to play?'"

She nodded. "'kay."

He hoped it worked. He worried how she'd feel if the kid she talked to *didn't* want to play.

"Ready to go into daycare now?"

She hopped off his lap and held her hand up. He took it and strode beside her into the building. Some of the children sat at small tables, coloring pictures. Others played with toys.

Luke squatted down. "Have fun today." He kissed her

cheek.

"Bye, Daddy." She stared at him for a few more seconds, then wandered toward a table, taking a seat.

She'd be at daycare for about a half-hour before getting on the school bus. She'd be fine. It couldn't be as bad as her first day. He was reluctant to leave, wanting to make sure she settled in.

His phone rang and he headed outside before answering. "Gary, I'll be there in five minutes. What couldn't wait?" He didn't want to hear the reason. Gary never called when Luke was on his way in, so it could only be bad news.

"Hey, Luke. I thought it was best to detour you to the scene. Jane's body was found this morning. It was dumped on the corner of her block, under some bushes."

Luke leaned against his car, a shiver racking his body. He'd only talked to her a few times, but of all the murder cases he'd worked on, this was the first one he knew the victim. His heart constricted, and he clutched his chest. And this psycho had come so close to taking Shannon. If a trained police officer couldn't escape, there wasn't much hope for any woman the killer might abduct.

Gary cleared his throat. "Two kids walking to school found her. Man, those poor kids are going to have nightmares for weeks."

"But, it hasn't even been a day. The pattern is different. Maybe it's not the same guy." As if hoping that someone else murdered her was any better.

"She got dumped nearly where she was taken. Of course, it's the same guy."

Luke ran a hand over his face. "You're probably right. I'm on my way." A cop's job had risks, but this death wasn't related to her job. It was about her hair color—whatever that symbol represented to the killer.

He arrived on site in minutes and parked near a small,

whispering crowd, craning their necks to see around the officers. The medical examiner's van stopped behind him. He got out and excused his way through the cluster of people. He ducked under the yellow tape and approached one of the uniformed officers. "Can't you disperse these people?"

"I tried. They aren't budging. This is as good as cops on TV for them."

Luke shook his head as he joined Gary near the bushes. Gary nodded at the ground and Luke squatted, lifting the tarp covering the body. He swore. He couldn't imagine how the kids reacted when they saw this.

The body was stretched out lying on its side, facing the street. Jane's lifeless eyes stared, as if accusing him of not saving her. He silently thanked her for what she'd done to save Shannon. He'd never had the chance while she was alive. He vowed to find the man who took her life.

Her hands had already been slipped into protective bags. The killer had cleaned the gash on the neck, making it easy to see it was deep. A difference from the other victims was that the top of the shirt was a bloody mess. She must have still been wearing it when her throat was cut. The other women appeared to have been redressed after being killed and washed. There were no strangulation bruises on Jane's throat.

It could be a copycat killer after all. So far, the similarities were red hair, a slashed throat, dumping the body close to where she was taken, and being kidnapped on a Wednesday.

Luke dropped the cover and moved to the side when the stretcher rolled up behind him.

The police photographer and video expert, Liz Barrett, stepped up and lifted the tarp. She grimaced. "Here. Hold one end. Allen, hold the other, so the crowd can't see her."

They took the corners, letting one edge touch the ground. A slight breeze blew, and Luke stepped on the corner of the tarp to keep it down.

Liz snapped a few photos—the whole body and some close-ups. With help from the coroner, she rolled the body forward. Luke's breath stuck in his throat when he saw the stab wound in the back. The other victims hadn't had that. Liz took more pictures before the body was bagged and removed.

Thoughts swirled through Luke's mind as he left for the station. It had been released to the public that these women died from a slash to the neck, and that they'd been returned near where they'd been abducted. They'd held back the strangulation, but pictures of all the victims attributed to the serial killer had been released. All had red hair. Jane's killer may be a copycat who took advantage of that. A perfect time to kill a cop would be when someone else got the blame.

~~~

In the middle of the afternoon, Luke visited the morgue, hoping the M.E. had completed the exam of Jane's body. He was anxious for any information on whether she was killed by the serial killer.

Sam leaned over the body that lay on the table, holding tweezers at the gash on the neck. His thick, black hair had a trace of gray at the temples, and magnifying glasses perched on his nose. He glanced over them as Luke entered.

"Hi, Sam. How's it going?"

"I'm not done yet, Luke." He glared and dropped his gaze back down to continue his examination.

"Can you tell me what you found so far?" Yeah, he was pushing, but his wheels were spinning with nothing to go on.

The older man rolled his eyes toward the ceiling, shook his head and sighed. He shoved his glasses to the top of his head with the back of his hand, rested his gloved hands on the table, and shrugged. "She wasn't raped. The stab wound on her back wasn't very deep. Between that and the angle, I think the weapon may have been thrown."

Luke straightened. "So, she might've been running?"

Sam shrugged. "Her knees are skinned, so that could indicate a fall while running. There's a bruise on the side of her jaw. It appears to be from a fist, but I still need to do more testing. There are scrapes on her knuckles that might be defensive wounds. And I still have to determine the characteristics of the knife. I can get more information from the back, since it plunged in, compared to the neck wound that slices across. So far, all I know is that the knife was sharp."

"So, it was the cut on the neck that killed her?"

Sam glared at him. "I'll know for sure later, but that's what it looks like so far. Don't hold me to it. And she wasn't strangled. At this point, she might not be a victim of your serial killer."

"The witness said that she was struggling with the killer and then went limp. Can you check for chloroform or something that might knock her out?"

"I've already sent in the tox screen, but most likely, if she was conscious, it cleared her system."

"All right. Thanks, Sam. Call me when you're finished." Luke headed back to the station and his lead detective.

Luke perched on the edge of Gary's desk. He'd been trying to piece together what might have happened to Jane. Had the killer chosen her because she was a cop with red hair or a woman with red hair? Maybe he was taunting them by killing one of their own, believing he was too smart to be caught.

He rubbed his hand down his face. "Jane wasn't raped."

Gary nodded. "Good. At least she didn't have to suffer that, too."

"I think she tried to escape, and he threw the knife at her. It didn't go deep enough to kill her, but it probably startled her, maybe giving the killer enough time to catch up. Then he probably panicked, yanked the knife out of her back and slashed her neck."

"So, you agree with me that it was the serial killer?" Gary asked.

Luke nodded. "It's him. My question now is, will Jane's murder satisfy him for another month? Or, is rape the biggest high for him? I wish I knew if he'll take another victim in the next couple days" He'd be extra vigilant with Shannon. For the next two days, he could follow her to work and be there when she left to go home. She wouldn't have to know.

Gary puffed out a breath. "It better be enough. We don't even have a good suspect list yet."

This death made it personal for the whole force, not that they hadn't been watching for anything suspicious, but now they would be extra vigilant. Jane's death was a huge loss for all of them.

Gary shoved back in his chair and kicked his desk. "I hope the next woman he tries to abduct puts a bullet in his brain."

Luke squeezed Gary's shoulder. Wishful thinking. If Jane didn't get a chance to do it, an untrained woman wouldn't have a chance.

Luke returned to his desk, and checked his email. He'd gotten a response from their video expert. He'd forwarded the security camera footage from Jane's house to Liz after checking it himself and not getting anything useful from it. He sure hoped she'd performed some magic. He dialed her number.

"Liz, it's Luke. Thanks for getting to this so fast."

"I had to do my best for Jane. I wish it could have been more." Her voice broke with the last.

He waited a couple of beats before continuing. He wished he could have done more, too, especially since Shannon blamed herself. "Did you find anything?"

"Not a lot. The video showed the car's a Lexus RX. Probably a 2019 to 2022. It's dark gray or black. I didn't get a plate number, and the assailant wore a ski mask."

He'd seen the mask, too. Luke wrote down the info. "Thanks. That eliminates a lot of cars. No dents are anything special on the car?"

"No. Sorry. Jane sure put up a good fight. I think she would have whipped his butt if he hadn't knocked her out. Luke, Jane trains—trained—women in self-defense, and she couldn't save herself." She sniffled. "You need to get this guy."

His gut wrenched. "We will, and every piece of information gets us one step closer. Maybe Gary can narrow this down to a manageable number of cars. Thanks, Liz."

Chapter 6

The next day, Luke got a call about a missing lifeguard at the public beach. Normally, an officer would have been dispatched, but he'd requested to be notified of missing women. He had nothing to go on yet, but he was afraid that their killer hadn't been satisfied with killing Jane.

He and Gary headed to the lake to question witnesses. The small building with a covered porch on the beach hadn't changed from years ago. He'd spent endless hours there with his friends, playing volleyball or roughhousing in the water, until a lifeguard blew their whistle. The lifeguards kept their belongings, life rings, paddles and other rescue items inside. Toward the back of the building, there was a door marked *Women*. A young man sat on the stand, leaning his elbows on his knees, watching a handful of swimmers.

A cute young woman, with her sun-streaked hair drawn back in a ponytail, paced barefoot in front of the building. She wore a large, bright pink t-shirt, her tan legs were bare.

Luke strode up to her. "I'm Detective Luke Cade, and this—" He gestured beside him. "—is Detective Gary Wassmann." He flipped his badge open.

"I'm Frankie Harris." Gray eyes studied him.

He pulled out his notebook. "Are you the one who called?"

She nodded.

"Why do you think Carrie Lawson is missing?"

"Carrie always gets here first." She fidgeted from one foot to the other and glanced toward the beach. "We're supposed to be at our posts at nine o'clock. She's usually here early. I've never arrived before her."

"Maybe she overslept or got a flat tire," Luke said.

She shook her head. "When I got here, the gate and building were already unlocked. Her car wasn't here, but sometimes her dad drops her off. I figured Carrie was inside, but she wasn't. So, then I thought that they'd forgotten to lock the door last night. But at ten after nine she still wasn't here, so I called and heard her phone ring inside her locker."

"Is that when you called us?" It didn't sound good, not when the girl was reliable and her belongs were present.

"Yeah. I was going to call her mom if she didn't answer, but I knew something was wrong when her phone was here."

He gestured toward the building. "Show me."

She led him inside. All the rescue items seemed to be in their proper places on hooks or stacked on the floor. The lockers were on the right wall at the back.

"Did it look like this when you got in?"

She shook her head. "One of the paddles was in the middle of the floor."

Four leaned into a corner near the door. Maybe this was where Carrie had been taken, and she tried to defend herself.

Frankie wiped tears from her cheeks, and spoke with a quiver in her voice. "I didn't think anything about it until her phone rang in the locker."

"Which locker is Carrie's?"

"This one." Frankie touched one. "Shall I open it?"

"You have the combination?"

"Yeah," She turned the dial and opened the locker. Inside, they found Carrie's purse, shorts and flip-flops.

"Do you have a picture of Carrie?" Luke asked

"Yeah, on my phone." She opened her locker and grabbed her phone. After a few seconds she showed it to Luke. A pretty girl with coppery red hair smiled at him. Red.

Hair. His gut clenched. He turned the screen toward his partner and Gary's grim expression became grimmer.

He handed the phone back. "Can you text me this picture?"

"Sure." He gave her the number, and she typed it into her phone. "There."

"Do you have Carrie's parent's phone number?"

"Yeah, we've got emergency contact numbers here." She pointed to a paper taped to the wall. Luke wrote down the numbers under Carrie's name.

"Thanks, Frankie. We'll do everything we can to find Carrie." Considering they didn't have any suspects, chances were slim.

He slipped on gloves and lifted each paddle, inspecting them for blood, hoping Carrie had gotten in a good whack before she was taken. Nothing. "I think we need to get these fingerprinted in case the killer yanked one from Carrie's hands.

"I'll call it in," Gary said.

Luke strode to where the sidewalk ended at the beach and stared across the lake. The houses on the other side were probably too far away for anyone to have seen someone abduct Carrie. Woods bordered both sides of the beach, so the only possible witness would be someone in the house across from the parking lot entrance. He'd see if anyone was home after the forensic team arrived.

His gaze strayed to the sand and water. He'd brought Shannon here. The times they jumped the gate after dark and skinny dipped were some of his fondest memories. They'd horseplay and he'd try to get her to scream. She worked hard not to because she didn't want the police to come and find her naked. He'd love to bring her back and create new memories. Maybe he could convince her into coming with him and Sherry, once he got her to talk to him. Wishful thinking.

He was a long way from that happening.

Luke sighed and headed back to the parking lot. Gary followed.

Gary leaned against the car. "It's him. I know it is."

Luke slammed his palm down on the car hood. "She's just a kid. We need to get this bastard."

~~~

Luke trudged beside Gary up the sandy, cement walk. He was saddened, but not surprised they were back at the beach. Two days ago, Carrie Lawson had been a missing person. Now she was victim number six. A female body, face up, lay half in the water. Frankie had been the unfortunate lifeguard to find her.

Frankie sat in a chair on the covered porch of the beach building, staring at her twisting hands. Today, she wore a lime green t-shirt. Luke stepped onto the porch and squatted down beside her. Tears streaked her cheeks.

Luke touched her knee. "Frankie, I'm sorry you had to be the one to find her."

She wiped the tears from her face and took a shuddering breath.

He covered her cold hand with one of his. "Did you go up to her?"

She nodded. "I didn't see her at first." She muffled a sob. "I opened up the building and then headed to the end of the beach. We do a quick once over for trash. Sometimes kids have parties at night. I was mostly staring at the sand and I didn't see her until I was almost on her."

Luke squeezed her hands, he hoped reassuringly. "Did you touch her?"

Frankie shook her head vigorously.

An old Honda Civic pulled into the lot. A teenage boy in

45

swim trunks and a t-shirt got out and sauntered up to them. "Hey, Frankie, what's going on?"

Frankie sobbed.

Luke stood and spoke quietly. "She found Carrie's body this morning."

The boy's eyes grew large, and he paled. "She's dead?"

Luke squeezed the young man's shoulder. "Yes. I'm sorry."

The boy took a step back, glanced toward the beach, and must have seen the body. His face paled and he wobbled. "Oh, my, God."

Luke sidestepped to block his view. "We're closing the beach for today. You might as well go home."

"What about Frankie?"

"She'll be leaving soon, too."

He nodded, and with one last glance at Frankie, headed back to his car.

Luke glanced at the body, and the rows of grooves in the sand. Maybe they'd gotten one small break. He squatted in front of the girl. "Frankie, when does the beach get raked?"

"We do it before we leave so trash doesn't blow around. We fill in holes that kids dig so anyone who comes in the dark doesn't trip on them."

"What time do you rake?"

"We kick everyone off the beach at seven. We're done by seven-thirty."

"Frankie, we're going to have to close the beach for the day. Can you go out to the road and inform people when they stop? When a police officer arrives, I'll have him take over, and you can go home."

"All right." She headed, at a slow pace, toward the parking lot entrance.

Luke and Gary tread carefully over the raked sand to the edge of the water. They stopped several feet short of the body. She wore the lifeguard swimsuit. Her hair, pulled back in a ponytail, was draped across one shoulder.

Frankie's footprints traveled parallel to the water from the left in the center of the beach, stopping short of the body by ten feet. A deeper, longer stride headed to the building. Frankie had run.

Two sets of footprints stretched between the water and the parking lot, one set deeper than the other. Luke squatted beside the body, their youngest victim so far. He'd failed her. She wouldn't go to college or get a regular job. She'd never marry or have children.

Shannon could have been found like this if it hadn't been for her self-defense training. He closed his eyes and willed away the images. He took a shuddering breath. That wasn't going to happen to her. He wouldn't let it.

From the waist down, Carrie lay in the gently lapping water. The body hadn't been thrown down or dropped. It had been placed exactly. Bruises circled the neck, as well as the killing gash. Bruises also marred the legs.

Luke stood and eyed the path of the footsteps. "Let's follow the tracks."

They paralleled the tracks from several feet away to the parking lot. "He was parked here," Luke said, pointing to a spot. "The tracks separate a couple of feet from the edge of the parking lot. I assume he took the body out of the trunk and walked straight down to the water. Then when he returned, he went directly to the driver's door." The dirt parking lot was too packed to see the tracks. "Maybe the forensic team can get something.

Luke crossed to Frankie at the entrance as she straightened up from a car that drove away. "Is this gate closed at night?"

"Yeah, we lock it when we leave. The first one here in the morning unlocks and opens it. That's another reason I thought Carrie was here the day she disappeared." She stared into the parking lot.

"Was it open this morning?"

"No. I unlocked it. That's why I didn't realize anything was wrong until I found Carrie." She blinked a few times, and covered her mouth.

Luke surveyed the scene. With shrubbery crowding the gate, no one could drive around the gate, and if they'd tried, the bushes would have been crushed.

"Who has keys to the gate?" Luke asked.

"All the lifeguards do. Alex Simpson, the head of the park commission. Maybe some other city workers."

"Thanks, Frankie."

Luke headed back to Gary, where he stood beside his car.

Luke leaned on his hand against the car. "The killer may have made a mistake." He explained to Gary about the gate.

"Maybe he picked the lock."

Luke sighed. "Could be, but let's check out everybody who could possibly have a key."

The M.E. drove into the lot and backed in beside Luke's car, followed by a police car.

The man got out of the van.

"Hey, Sam," Luke said.

"Luke, Gary, I'm seeing way too much of you two."

Luke huffed out a breath. "We're doing the best we can. We don't want to see your face either."

Officer Martin Shay clapped Luke on the back. "Tough job to come back to."

"It's what I signed up for. Marty, can you relieve the lifeguard? Have her unlock the padlock so you can lock up when everybody leaves."

"Sure thing." He headed in Frankie's direction.

"Sam, I'll take you down to the body." He glanced at

Gary. "Bring down the rest of the gang when they get here."

Luke pointed to the two sets of tracks. "Those most definitely belong to the killer."

Another car stopped behind him, and a door opened and closed.

"Luke, wait for me," Liz said.

Gary grabbed Liz's arm, causing her camera to swing out and smack him on the hand.

"See those prints?"

She nodded, staring down at them.

"Those were made by the killer. Don't mess them up."

She yanked her arm out of his grasp and glared at him. "This isn't my first rodeo. I'll just grab some pictures of these, then I'll join them at the body."

At the click of the camera's shutter, Luke headed back to the water.

Sam's kakis and crisp white shirt were more out of place on the beach than Luke's jeans and short sleeved buttondown shirt.

Sam pointed at the neck. "That matches the other bodies."

They stepped back to let Liz take pictures.

Luke stopped her from stepping too close. "Careful of the footprints."

She glared at him, pointed her camera at one of the prints and clicked a few shots. "The prints are crisper here in the wet sand."

"That's why I have the molds," chimed in one of the men.

Luke glanced up, "Hey, Dave."

Dave dropped his bucket of materials a couple of feet from the tracks and took a step closer. "From all the footprints, I think the guy took his time getting the body just right."

The tracks stayed on one side of the body and at the head.

Luke pointed to two rounded depressions in the sand beside the waist. "Hey, do you think he dropped onto his knees when he laid the body down?"

"Looks like it. I'll get casts of those, too. Maybe we can determine height by distance from his feet to knees."

Luke took a step back. "I think I'm done here. I want reports as soon as you've finished."

He headed for the parking lot, and Gary fell in beside him. They reached their cars, and Luke studied the surroundings. "Why would the killer open the gate to dump the body at the water's edge? He could have left it at the street, but he took an extra risk to go all the way to the water."

Gary shrugged. "Maybe he thinks he's infallible, and he's taunting us."

"I'm going to talk to the neighbors to see if anyone saw anything. I want you to find out who has keys. Then we'll split up the list and find out where those people were during each kidnapping and dump."

He canvassed the street. One woman had seen a car drive up to the gate, and a man with dark hair opened it and drove in. A man walking his dog at three in the morning had seen the car in the lot. One small piece of new information, the man had dark hair.

The killer was too illusive, which meant Shannon was still in danger.

Chapter 7

On Saturday, Luke ran with Shannon. The last couple times, Shannon allowed him to run beside her partway into the run, but this wasn't one of those mornings. That was all right with Luke because he was ready to follow her into her house. The past three runs, he had completed the loop a second time. He wouldn't let her lock him out this time.

She sped up as they approached her house, but this time Luke stayed right behind her. Halfway to the door, she glanced over her shoulder.

"What are you doing, Luke?" She ran up the steps and stopped.

Luke crowded her. "We're going to talk."

"No. We're not."

He pulled the key from her hand, and unlocked the door. He grabbed her hand and tugged her inside, and to the couch. "Sit."

Shannon yanked her hand from his grasp, crossed her arms, and glared. She was never one to yell. He almost wished she would. It would be some kind of dialogue.

Luke crowded her. "Please sit."

Shannon glared at him for endless seconds, then sat in the center of the couch. Luke sat on the arm, but when she stared up at him, he decided he didn't want to tower over her and slid down to the seat. She scooted a little away from him. He wanted to take her hand, but she wouldn't let him. He didn't want to turn this into a power play. Any more of one than it already was. It was already going to be difficult.

Shannon stared at her hands, laced in her lap.

He drew in a deep breath. "Shannon, I'm sorry I hurt you four years ago. I didn't realize how much until I saw you again. I remembered you tried to say something when I came to tell you I was leaving, but I didn't let you speak. I couldn't say what I needed to if you interrupted me."

Shannon didn't say anything as she held her body rigid. Once again, Luke stopped himself from reaching out to her.

"Shannon, tell me what you were trying to say."

She glared at him. "You're not important to me anymore, so you don't need to know."

He closed his eyes as the pain sliced into him. He deserved it, but he didn't believe her. She wouldn't be upset after all this time if he wasn't important. He lowered his voice. "Maybe telling me will give you closure." He hoped that wouldn't be the result.

Her face was pinched with pain. "And did you get *closure* telling me about that woman you went off to marry?"

"No. It wasn't like that."

She glanced up at him with tears shimmering in her eyes. "You know what? I didn't hear it anyway, beyond you telling me you were marrying that woman." Her gaze dropped back down again.

Luke was almost surprised that Shannon had said anything to him. So, all that time he'd spent coming up with exactly what to say was wasted because she didn't hear more than the first few sentences. She hadn't heard him tell her he still loved her. But would that have mattered? He was leaving her for another woman. He hadn't expected her to be devastated. He should have, but at that point, he was only thinking about how he could fix one problem. He didn't think about the consequences of his actions.

"Can you tell me what you would have said?" he asked softly.

She shook her head, and stared at her hands. "It doesn't matter now."

"Shannon, you don't know how much I regret doing this the way I did. I'm sorry I cut you off. I think I need to hear your thoughts." He waited, hoping the silence would force her to speak. Several minutes passed, and he began to wonder if he should get up and leave.

"I was excited and scared when you arrived." Her voice was so low he almost didn't hear the words.

Scared? Did she already know what he was going to say? She couldn't have. She wouldn't have let him in if she had.

A few tears ran down her cheeks. Luke wanted to wipe them from her face, but couldn't. She'd probably kick him out. "Why were you excited and scared?"

She shook her head, her eyes closed. "I can't."

"Please, Shannon." This was important. She needed to say it. He waited, wanting to touch her, encourage her.

"I was pregnant." She turned her back to him.

Was? He felt like his heart stopped then was ripped out of his chest. He'd abandoned her when she was pregnant. He covered his eyes. He wished they could live that day over, and he'd let Shannon speak. Their lives would be so different now. His eyes clouded, and he blinked.

"Shannon, I don't understand. You were pregnant?" A hundred questions raced through his mind, but he held them back, afraid she'd lock herself in the bathroom, and then he wouldn't find out anything more. The hardest thing to do was to wait.

"For weeks after you left, I was such a mess. Then I decided I had to pull myself together because I'd have to take care of a baby alone."

A knife twisted in his heart because he'd put her in that position.

She barely got the next words out because she was sobbing. "And then…I lost the baby."

"Oh, Shannon." She'd gone through losing their baby alone, without him by her side. She'd probably hit him, but Luke had to hold her. He slid closer and wrapped his arms around her waist, loose enough that she could free herself if she needed to.

"The doctor said it was stress."

A chill shivered through him and squeezed his heart so hard he thought it might stop beating. It was *all* his fault. His fault she was pregnant. His fault she'd been all alone. His fault she'd miscarried. No wonder she hated him. She'd never be able to forgive him.

Shannon's cries turned to sniffles, and Luke slowly released her. He slid back to put some space between them. He'd intended on telling her about Annie, but was too overwhelmed to say anything. He needed time to deal with the loss of a child who'd died before it was born. "I think we both need a little time before we talk more. Will you be okay if I leave now?"

Her head remained bowed, but she nodded. Luke stood and kissed the top of her head, then left the house, making sure to lock the door behind him.

~~~

Telling Luke about the baby had exhausted Shannon. She tipped her head against the back of the couch and pulled in a deep breath. It eased something inside her now that Luke knew. Why after four years, it should make a difference, she wasn't sure. It still hurt that she'd lost the baby, but now Luke understood the multiple ways he'd hurt her.

Thank God for Will. She couldn't have asked for a better brother. He was the only reason she made it through. He forced her to go out. He took her out for pizza. He took her to the baseball games he coached. He invited her to dinner with Leah and the kids. None of her friends had been able to get through to her. Will took charge. She hadn't wanted to do any of those things, but they were exactly what she needed to start living again.

She didn't need Luke in her life. It was easier and less complicated without him. Maybe she should do her morning run at the high school. It meant getting up earlier to drive to the track and back, and the monotony of running circles with no change in scenery.

Shaking her head, she fisted her hands. She was making excuses to still see Luke. No. She just didn't want him to mess up her routine.

With the killer still out there, she couldn't go out and run off her agitation, so she paced in her living room. She passed the window, seeing Luke's car still in front of her house, his seat tipped back, and all that was visible was his arm draped over his face. He was probably upset about what she'd told him. He deserved to be since it was all his fault.

~~~

Luke sat in his car in front of Shannon's house, too upset to drive. He put the seat back and covered his eyes with his arm. He knew he'd treated Shannon badly, but he ached at finding out how truly horrible he'd been. It was no wonder she hadn't wanted to see or talk to him. His pain at abandoning Shannon and the loss of their baby couldn't compare with how she'd suffered at his hands. She'd trusted him, and he'd left her when she needed him most.

Now he understood why she'd panicked when he showed up at her door. He expected that she'd gotten over him, moved on. Maybe even gotten married. That thought made his heart ache. He'd been shocked that she'd acted afraid of him and ran.

Now he knew why. He'd ruined probably years of her life. Maybe, even now, he still tormented her by trying to get back with her.

Luke let out a growl and sat his seat up. He wouldn't figure out anything like this. He drove home.

He trudged into the kitchen where his mother washed breakfast dishes.

Surprise crossed her face. "You look like hell."

"Thanks, Mom."

"Daddy!" His daughter barreled out of her room and hugged his legs. The blue eyed, blonde was the image of her mother. What would his other child have looked like? Would Sherry have been friends with her two-years-younger brother or sister?

"Hi, sprite. Would you mind playing in your room for a little bit longer while I talk to Grandma? Then we'll go do something fun."

"'Kay." She took two steps and turned back. "But not very long, please."

Luke would normally laugh at Sherry's wheedling expression, but his heart was too heavy. "I'll try, honey."

He dropped into a kitchen chair, and propped his elbows on the table, squeezing his temples between his fingers and circled them.

Elaine dried her hands and joined him. She folded her hands on the table and leaned forward, waiting for him to start.

"Shannon talked to me today. Did you know she was pregnant when I left?"

"I didn't know until she miscarried."

"Why didn't you tell me?"

She dropped her shoulders. She'd lost a grandchild only

a couple of months after finding out about her first grand-child. "It wasn't my place, and it was already difficult for you."

"I wouldn't have left her if I'd known. And it's my fault I didn't know because I wouldn't let her tell me." His own words caused him pain. Why hadn't he discussed the situation with her? Maybe she would have seen something he hadn't. But he'd jumped to one course of action and steam-rolled to the end.

"Did she tell you the rest?"

His chest went hot, then cold. He fisted his hands and thumped them on the table. "There's more?"

"Did she tell you the circumstances of her miscarriage?" Elaine bit her lip. "Maybe I should let her tell you this too."

He frowned, leaning closer. "She said it was caused by stress. Was there more to it?"

"She nearly lost her life."

Someone must have dumped ice water over his head. His heart beat erratically. Shannon had nearly died. And he hadn't been there for her. Could it get any worse? The reasons for her to hate him kept piling higher and higher. The walls she'd build against him were created with layers and layers of pain. "What happened?" The words choked him.

"Will checked on her frequently. One day he called her at work, and she wasn't there, so he went to her apartment. When she didn't answer the door, he used his key and let himself in. He found her on the floor in a pool of blood. If he'd been an hour or two later, she wouldn't have made it. As it was, it was touch and go for a while. They nearly had to do a hysterectomy."

"That's what Will meant when he said she nearly didn't survive the first time I abandoned her. I thought he meant she was either an emotional wreck, or she'd tried to commit suicide." Without Will, Shannon wouldn't be here today.

Luke folded his arms on the table and dropped his head down. Elaine rested her hand on his shoulder. Shannon could have died or never be able to have children. They'd talked about wanting kids. Finally, he raised his head and sat back. "I can't believe how much of a disaster I caused, just because I thought I was doing the right thing."

He clenched his hand. "And the long speech I gave to Shannon telling her why I had to leave, was worthless. She didn't hear anything after I said I was leaving. I might as well have left her a note that simply said good-bye."

"Give it time, Luke. At least now you know what you're dealing with."

"And it seems hopeless. Why would she want someone back who professed to love her but left. And was the cause of her losing our baby and nearly dying. She'll never trust me again." He closed his eyes and dropped his head.

"She talked to you, so it's a step in the right direction. Now you have a chance."

"You think so?"

"Better than last week, anyway." She smiled and stood. "Now, I'm going home."

He'd thought he could drop back into her life and talk her into spending time with him, let him convince her he wasn't the same man who left her. But sometimes a scar went so deep it couldn't be healed.

But he couldn't give up. She was the only woman he'd ever loved. Now to find a way to prove it.

Chapter 8

On Monday morning Luke made calls. First, he left a message for the M.E. "Hey, Sam. It's Luke. Let me know if you got anything from Carrie Lawson's autopsy."

He dialed the next number. His case had been given priority over all others, so any evidence he sent to forensics would be tested first. "Hey, Dave. It's Luke."

"Luke, I was going to call you later."

"Does that mean you have something for me?" Luke needed some good news from someone.

"Well, the shoes aren't special, expensive, one-of-a-kind shoes, if that's what you mean. There's a cut across one of the soles. So, if you happen to have a suspect, you can check his shoes for the cut."

"Well, that's something. Now, we just need a suspect." Or a bunch of them, so they could start eliminating.

"We've got a good set of knee prints, so that's another comparison you can make when the time comes. I tried all kinds of calculations between the knees and toes, but couldn't figure out a height. There are too many variables. Sorry."

"So, nothing to help me now?"

"Not really. But there's one more thing. We got a partial print on her bracelet. It's not hers, and it might not be the killer's. It's also not complete enough to run it, but if you have a suspect, you can try for a match."

"Thanks, Dave." Luke put the phone down, and rubbed his eyes. This killer was so careful. Luke was beginning to think they'd never find him. No! He'd make another mistake, and they'd catch him.

The killer had messed up twice. He underestimated Shannon, and she'd gotten away. He'd underestimated Jane Roslin, and she'd almost gotten away.

Gary sauntered up to his desk, sat on the edge and handed him a paper. "Here's your list. I think we can eliminate the women."

Luke scanned the page. "What's this?"

"Your half of the list of gate key owners for the past five years."

Luke shook his head. "Women, too."

Gary raised his eyebrows. "You think a woman could have done this?"

"No. I think a husband, boyfriend or brother could have taken a woman's key."

"Ah, gotcha. I'll keep that in mind." He took a few steps. "Were your other serial killer cases this hard?"

"Hard in what way?"

Gary frowned. "You know, the elusive killer, and dealing with all these deaths."

"Yeah, deaths of innocent people are always hard to deal with. My first case, the killer was pretty sloppy and left clues every time. We just had to put the pieces together. The second one was harder. It's like this one, in that the killer is pretty careful. We ended up getting a lucky break." Luke slumped back in his chair. "I sure hope this killer screws up soon."

"Here's hoping. I'll get you an updated list in a few minutes." Gary raised his list in a salute and walked away.

Luke studied his list. The mention of keys made him wonder if Carrie's key to the gate was with her belongs cleared out from her locker. Maybe the killer had taken it with him. He hadn't thought to check when he was there the other day. If it was missing, they wouldn't need to go through the list of key owners. He folded the paper and tucked it into his shirt pocket. He could grab lunch on his way back.

At the evidence room, Luke signed out Carrie's keys. One looked like it belonged to a padlock, but he'd have to test it to be sure.

Luke drove to the beach and found an empty space at the end of the parking lot. Apparently, a body being dumped in the water didn't stop people from wanting to swim. He headed to the gate, shoved the suspect key in the lock and turned it. The killer didn't steal it or had picked the lock. Their search might be a total waste of time.

Since he was already there, he might as well talk to the lifeguards and see if they had anything more to add. A guy sat in the closer stand, and the blonde ponytail of the woman on the second indicated it was Frankie. He trudged through the hot sand, wishing he could take off his jacket, but not wanting to show his gun.

Today, a red t-shirt was draped over the back of her seat. He stopped in front of her, and she continued to stare intently over the water, sunglasses covering her pretty gray eyes.

He tipped his head up, shielding his eyes from the sun. "Hi, Frankie."

She dropped her gaze to him then focused back on the water. "What can I do for you, Detective Cade?"

She jumped up, blew her whistle and screamed, "No horse play!" She sat back down.

Luke scanned the water and spotted a group of boys separate. "That's amazing."

"Well, if they don't behave, they get kicked out of the water for the day. I've done it to a couple of them before, so they know I'm serious."

Luke was surprised how loud she yelled. "Could Carrie

yell as loud as you?"

Her eyebrows dropped. "Well, yeah." Stupid question.

Luke wondered if Carrie had screamed for help and if anyone in the area had heard her. He still had to canvas the neighborhood in the evening.

"Frankie, where do you keep your key when you're not here?"

She glanced at him and back to the water. "It's always in my purse. Why?"

"The killer opened the padlock. Maybe he had a key. Does anyone have access to your key?"

Her head snapped to him and her mouth dropped open. It was several seconds before her gaze returned to the water.

"Only my mother. You don't think she did it, do you?"

"No. Thanks, Frankie."

Luke trudged over to the other lifeguard. He wasn't the same one they'd sent home on the day Carrie's body was found. This boy's shoulders were wider, like he lifted weights. His hair was a bit shaggy. He had an arrogant expression that screamed girl magnet.

Luke climbed up a couple rungs, introduced himself and asked the boy his name.

"Jake Steiger. Is this about Carrie?"

"Yeah. Since the killer opened the gate, I'm tracking down the keys to the padlock. Does anyone else have access to your key?"

Jake wasn't quite as diligent as Frankie. He didn't glance back at the water as they talked. "Just my roommate. I leave everything from my pockets on my dresser."

"What's your roommate's name?"

"He wouldn't have done this."

"Probably not. But we have to track down everything."

"Matt Hickock."

Luke pulled out his paper and wrote it down.

"Who opened this morning?"

"Frankie did."

"Can we check to see if your key is still in your locker?"

Jake nodded. He called out to Frankie and told her he'd be gone a couple of minutes. Luke climbed down and Jake jumped from the top. Once inside the building, Jake opened his locker, fished his keys from his shorts pocket and held his hand open. He tipped up one key. "Here it is."

Luke nodded. "You weren't working the morning Carrie's body was discovered. Could anyone have gotten hold of your key that morning?"

Jake shook his head. "No. My roommate and his girlfriend were away for a few days. In fact, they just got back last night."

"All right, I think we're done for now. Thanks." Luke pulled out the list.

"You know, there are a lot of keys out there."

Luke studied Jake. His list was as long as Gary's, so that was true, but he wanted to hear Jake's comment. "What do you mean?"

"Well, some people don't return their keys at the end of the season. They think they'll be back the next summer to guard and then they aren't. Some keys get lost and they're issued new ones." He shrugged and walked away.

Luke stared after him. He wondered how often the padlock was changed. He assumed previous lifeguards were on the list, but he hadn't considered them losing keys. A key could be in the hands of someone not on the list and not related to someone on the list. He wrote down what he'd learned. It wasn't encouraging.

Luke decided to stop by the M.E.'s office before going back to the station. Sam sat at his desk typing on his keyboard.

"Hey, Sam. I'm glad I caught you."

The M.E. glanced up. "I see you got my message."

Luke frowned. "No. I just decided to stop by. What's up?"

"I was catching up on my reports and realized that I hadn't told you about the knife used on Jane Roslin."

Luke sat in the chair in front of Sam's desk. "What about it?"

"Remember how she was the only victim who was stabbed?"

Luke nodded.

"The wound was probably made by an X-Acto blade. That's one reason it didn't penetrate deep."

Luke dropped his shoulders. "Almost everyone has one in their house. Every clue we find is no help at all."

"Also, I didn't detect any drugs or chemicals in Jane Roslin's blood."

"Did you find anything on Carrie Lawson?"

"Same as the others. The bruising from strangulation appears to be the same size hands. She was raped, but there was no trace of semen."

A senseless death and no new clues.

Chapter 9

Two weeks after the devastating news of Shannon's miscarriage, Luke ran behind her once again, allowing her the distance she needed during their runs. She might not be ready to talk to him again, but he finally was. It'd taken time for him to come to terms with the loss of a baby he hadn't known about. The loss cut even deeper, knowing that it might not have happened if he'd been there for her. The pain of leaving Shannon was nothing compared to the agony of how Shannon had suffered alone.

Her legs pumped, moving her smoothly forward. He remembered her telling him about being on the track team in high school, and the high she felt at competitions. Did she feel that same high, making sure she stayed ahead of him, as they ran through the park? More likely, it was desperation to make sure he wouldn't talk to her. He hoped someday they'd run side by side again, as they had when they'd dated.

As always, he kept his gaze moving. He was familiar enough with the route to search out the hiding places. They occasionally passed other runners or walkers.

It seemed as if Shannon had been running faster at the end to make sure Luke couldn't follow her into her house again. This time he'd have to convince her to let him in. They needed this conversation, no matter how much she didn't want to hear it. Maybe hearing it would make it hurt less. Maybe. It was one more thing they had to clear up in order to get Shannon back, or at least, to give her peace.

After they crossed the street, Luke sped up so he ran beside her, his arm bumping hers. She frowned at him. They ran up her steps and stood in front of the door. She glared at him. "Luke, what are you doing?"

"We need to talk."

Shannon shook her head. "No, we don't." She slid the elastic key cord off her arm with trembling fingers. "Go away."

"I listened to you last time. I need you to listen to me, too."

"Like you should have done four years ago?"

Luke grimaced. "Yes. Like how I should have listened to you. I regret that with everything in me. As much as I'd like to, I can't change what I did four years ago." He had to make her understand why he'd done what he had. "I'm sorry, Shannon. But I do need you to listen to me and maybe you'll understand."

After agonizing minutes of Shannon studying him, Luke was pretty sure she'd tell him to leave. Finally, she sighed heavily and nodded.

~~~

"I don't know why I'm putting myself through this." She stormed into the house, already regretting letting him in. Luke closed the door.

He didn't respond, probably knowing she'd change her mind if he said the wrong thing. There wasn't anything he could say that would make it better. She shouldn't even bother. It would have been so much better if Luke had asked someone else to run with her. She could have insisted, or gone to the high school to run, but she hadn't. Did she want him near her? No. Maybe.

She sat at the end of the couch, not wanting to hear what he had to say, but he seemed to think it would make a difference. She sighed. He was here now. Let him have his say.

He sat at the other end of the couch and narrowed his eyes, staring for so long, she was about to tell him to leave. Maybe he was trying to gauge her reaction. He used to be good at it.

"I met Annie when I was five and she was four. Our parents had been friends for years, and when the house next door went up for sale, her parents bought it. Annie was like my little sister."

Anger boiled her blood. "Brothers don't get their sisters pregnant."

Luke took a deep breath. "I'm getting to that." He rubbed his forehead. "When we were in high school, they moved away. It was a three-hour drive, so we didn't see much of each other after that. Then her parents died in a small plane crash. I was twenty. My parents and I went there to help her out. They invited her to stay with us as long as she needed to. She refused. Her parents had left her the house and a large life insurance policy. We stayed with her for a couple of weeks. She seemed to be doing all right."

Luke leaned back, his gaze on her. She wondered what he'd say next and reminded herself she didn't want to hear it.

"One night I heard Annie crying. I let myself into her room to see if I could help. She told me that she was supposed to be on the plane with her parents. She was upset that she hadn't died with them. I told her that their last thoughts were probably of her and how relieved they must have been she hadn't gone with them. I tried my best to comfort her and…" Luke's face reddened, and he glanced away from Shannon. "One thing led to another, and we had sex."

He took a deep breath and looked back at her. "It was the only time it happened."

Shannon glared at Luke, then dropped her gaze to her laced fingers. A twenty-year-old trying to soothe a girl he'd known his whole life, while in her bed. She wasn't surprised at what had happened. At least, it was before they were dating.

"I hadn't seen her for over three years when she showed up on my doorstep with a toddler in tow."

Shannon shook her head and stared at a picture of her and her brother on the wall. Will had shocked her with the news that Luke had a daughter who had become friends with Willa.

She didn't want to hear how Luke realized he loved Annie. She started to stand, and Luke lunged across the couch. He pulled her down beside him. "Shannon, please." His voice caught. "It's not what you think."

"I don't know if I can," she choked out. She kept her face averted.

Luke continued anyway. "I was floored when Annie told me that Sherry was my daughter. She hadn't told me she was pregnant because she hadn't wanted to burden me with a child when she was the one who pushed for us to have sex."

Luke took another deep breath. "Before I had time to recover from finding out I was a father, Annie told me she was dying of pancreatic cancer. The doctors told her she probably had six months left. She wouldn't be able to take care of her daughter, so she wanted me to take Sherry."

His arm tightened around Shannon. It might be hard for him to talk about Annie, but it was hard for her to hear, too. A heavy weight pressed on her chest. The thought reverberated that Luke had chosen Annie over her.

"Annie was going to leave Sherry with me and go back to her home to die alone. We'd been friends since we were little kids. I tried to convince her to stay here, but she refused. She wanted to go back to her parents' house. So, I told her we'd get married, and I'd take care of both of them. No woman should have to spend her last six months alone, without her child."

Luke gazed at her, and touched her cheek. "I didn't think. I was overwhelmed by Annie's situation. I wanted to make sure she was treated right."

"You could have become her health proxy."

He shrugged. "I didn't know about them back then, and how could I have done it without moving there?"

Shannon didn't want to listen, but the pain in his voice and on his face wrenched at her. Was it for Annie? Or her?

"We got married by a judge, and I moved into her house. I started on the police force there."

Luke leaned back, away from Shannon. He stared into her eyes and touched her cheek again. "A couple of months later, I told Annie about you. She was angry, and said she wouldn't have married me if she'd known." He dropped his hand back to his leg.

Even Annie thought it was wrong. If circumstances had been different, Shannon might have liked Annie. She'd had the toughest of situations to deal with, and given all the facts, would have refused Luke's solution.

His eyes became unfocused. "Annie got worse, and then she was offered an experimental treatment. If it didn't kill her, she had a chance for a cure. She'd been in a lot of pain and was ready to die, but decided that even if the treatment didn't work, it could help other cancer victims." He sighed. "Annie was cured, healthy and happy for almost three years."

Luke rubbed his forehead. "I figured, six months, I could do. Now, would it be my whole life? I felt guilty because before, I'd have been with her for *her* whole short life. When she was healthy, she actually urged me to come back to you. I wanted to, but I'd promised to take care of both of them. I couldn't leave my daughter. She'd become a part of me. And I couldn't take her from her mother. I'd committed to them both, and although I wasn't in love with Annie, I cared for her. I felt trapped."

Trapped because he'd never given Shannon a chance to give her input. Maybe together they could've convinced Annie to move near Luke.

Luke glanced at Shannon for a moment before his eyes locked on her and Will's picture. "She got to see her daughter grow. Sherry had a mother who loved her. When the cancer returned, it was more aggressive than before, and Annie died two months later."

Pain filled Luke's eyes. She could imagine how hard it would be to watch someone you cared for die painfully. But it still didn't lessen her pain because he'd left her. Shannon had suffered a painful loss too. She understood better, but if he'd loved her enough, he would have discussed Annie's problem with her. They could have figured out something together, even if it was to move closer to Annie. Shannon couldn't get past that she was Luke's second choice, and she didn't know if she could live with that.

"I cleared up everything there and sold the house, then I moved back here with Sherry."

"Why did you come back?"

She caught the pain in his eyes again as he locked them on her. The two of them deserved sorrow, but her pain was real, too, and he was the cause.

"Because I want us to have another chance. Shannon, I still love you."

"But you married her." That was the part that hurt the most. "You discuss a life changing decision with the one you love, and you didn't. You made a choice without even thinking of how it would affect me. With the two of us, and even Annie, too, we might've come up with a solution that satisfied everyone."

She and Luke had started to talk about a life together, but he'd destroyed it all without a thought of her feelings.

Luke closed his eyes for a second. "I just didn't give myself enough time to think it through. I'm sorry." He sighed.

"Instead, you went off and lived with her for four years."

"Like a brother."

"Like you were her brother when you got her pregnant?"

"Shannon." He sounded worn out. "That was the only time we had sex."

"What? You never had sex with your wife?" How could he live in the same house with the woman he created a child with and not have sex with her?

"We had separate bedrooms. I was coming back to you after…And I just couldn't see her that way." Luke touched her cheek. "The last time I made love was with you."

Shannon turned her head away, freeing her of his fingers, as the last time Luke made love to her flashed through her mind. It was a surprise when he showed up at her apartment just after she got home from work, with dinner in an actual picnic basket. They went to the beach and spread a blanket on the sand. He pulled out the take-out trays from Little Louie's, her favorite restaurant, but not his. In the bottom was a bottle of wine and two plastic glasses. She laughed, expecting to see sandwiches and sodas. It smelled heavenly. They enjoyed their meal while talking and watching the sunset over the trees on the far shore. Afterward, they drove back to her apartment and made love, and not for the first time, Luke told her he loved her. Two days later, he was gone.

She blinked back tears, not wanting him to see her cry. "Is that the end of your story?"

He sighed. "Yes. I'll let myself out." He stood over her for almost a minute, shoulders dropped, and eyes almost vacant. Maybe he thought she'd change her mind. He shuffled to the door, and it clicked behind him.

Shannon leaned back against the couch. She picked up a throw pillow and hugged it tightly as her tears flowed. Knowing Luke hadn't loved Annie romantically didn't help. It still meant Annie had been more important to him than she was.

If he'd loved her like he said he did, why hadn't he come to her to figure it out? Instead, he announced his intentions to marry another woman. He hadn't given them a chance. Without a thought about her feelings, he chose the other woman. Where did that leave her? His actions proved he hadn't loved her enough. Otherwise, he wouldn't have left her the way he did.

She pitched the pillow across the room, knocking the picture of Will and her off the wall. It hit a table, shattering the glass. Like her life. Shattered again.

~~~

Luke climbed into his car, rolled the windows down, and tipped the seat back. He hadn't expected the exhaustion that followed telling Shannon about Annie. It'd been hard to watch a dear friend suffer and almost die. Then there was the thrill when she'd gone into pain free remission, only to watch her three years later go through the pain again.

A different guilt had assailed him when Annie recovered. She should have had a husband who could love and want her the way she deserved. Instead, the part of his heart she needed belonged to Shannon. When Annie had regained her vitality, she'd come on to him a few times. He felt revulsion, made an excuse and left the house for a few hours. They never discussed why he disappeared, but she knew the reason. After that, they fell back into their old patterns, as if they were siblings.

He'd been considering divorce, for both their sakes. If

he'd acted on it sooner, he might have been gone when her cancer returned. And then, more guilt had hammered him. He'd almost broken his promise to not leave her to die alone.

The one shining star through that time had been his little sprite. He'd fallen in love with his daughter the moment he'd seen her. She'd taken to him immediately, as if she felt their connection. He was glad that she had more time with her mother.

He might never get Shannon back. His heart twisted. He hadn't realized how much he loved her until she was no longer a part of his life. They both suffered because he screwed up, but Shannon's suffering had been worse than his.

If it hadn't happened the way it did, Sherry might not have had as much time with her mother. If he'd convinced Annie to move close to him, would she have found out about the experimental treatment? As much as he hated that he and Shannon might never get back together, he wouldn't ex-change it for Sherry having three more years with her moth-er.

He took a deep breath and slowly let it out. Relief washed over him that Shannon now knew the whole story about Annie. He'd known she wouldn't immediately fall into his arms and forgive him, especially after he found out about the baby they'd lost. He didn't know if he could convince Shannon that he loved her and wouldn't leave again, but he wasn't giving up, even if they had no chance.

Chapter 10

Monday morning, Luke wove his way through groups of two to four officers, takeout cup in hand. The smell of burnt coffee made him glad he'd taken the time to pick up his own. He nodded to a couple of men.

Gary's voice stopped Luke as he passed the man's desk. "Luke, you'll never guess what happened."

Gary grabbed a paper off his desk. "Let's talk in your office."

Luke frowned as Gary followed him, closing the door behind them.

A smug smile covered Gary's face. "Jordan Ford's suitcase came into the station."

Luke sat in his chair and leaned back, lifting one corner of his mouth. "It just walked in?"

"With a little help. I was here yesterday when this homeless man walked in with it. He told Jackson he thought it was Jordan's. So, Jackson called me, and I brought the guy into an interview room." Gary leaned back in his chair, and crossed his arms. "His name's Jimmy Taylor. Late Friday night, he was tucked into one of the doorways in the factory area, and heard a car door close. He peeked around the edge, and saw a man throw something into a dumpster. After the guy left, Jimmy checked it out. He found a suitcase right on top, and grabbed it. He opened it, and found women's clothes—" Gary smiled widely. "—but he also found a letter addressed to Jordan Ford tucked into a pocket. That's when he decided we needed to see it. He said if it was his daughter, he'd want someone to do that."

Luke leaned on his elbows. "Did you dust it for prints?"

Gary's face fell. "Yeah, but only Jordan's and Jimmy Taylor's showed up."

"Did he get a plate number or give you a description of the guy?"

Gary grinned. "Seven-five. He said he couldn't see the rest of the plate because of the angle. Meredith Somers caught a seven also. I think it's the same car."

"What did he have to say about the guy?"

"White guy, black or very dark hair, shorter than collar length but not a crew cut. He only got a look at the profile. The guy had a very prominent chin and no facial hair."

Luke tensed. "Finally, a lead. Did you run the plate?"

Gary dropped his paper in front of Luke and slammed his palm on it. He smiled. "I highlighted the ones that are dark colored, medium sized, four-door Lexus. There are forty-one in the county."

"It could be a stolen plate," Luke said.

Gary shrugged. "He wouldn't keep the plate that long."

Luke would love to talk to every one of these car owners, look in the eyes of the guy who almost took Shannon's life. But, there wasn't enough time to do it all himself.

"Give me a third of the list, you take a third, and give the rest to someone you trust."

Gary nodded. "Wyatt can do it."

Luke stood and leaned his hand on the desk. "Let me know of anyone who's the least bit suspicious, and I'll check them out further. Tell that to Wyatt." He took the list Gary held out.

Gary stood. "Not a problem. Anything doesn't sound right, I'll hand it over. Oh, and I'm about halfway through the padlock key list."

Luke nodded. "Good." He glanced at the new list, then

fished in a drawer, pulling out his own key list. He compared the lists and found one name in common, marking it on both sheets.

He sorted through them by distance. He'd talk to the ones in town first and work his way out. Some of the cars were owned by women, but that didn't mean that men didn't drive them.

~~~

No one was home at the first two addresses Luke visited. He'd have to go back in the evening. Luke pulled into the driveway of the third house. All the houses in the upper-middle-class neighborhood were well maintained. A gray-haired man with wire rimmed glasses answered his knock. Luke introduced himself. "Are you George Barton?"

"Yes, what can I do for you, detective?"

He seemed curious and not nervous. He was also too old to have committed the murders. "Do you own a black Lexus RX, Mr. Barton?"

"Yes, I do." His curiosity turned to a frown.

"May I have a look at it, sir?"

The man's eyebrows popped up. "Sure, it's in the garage." He stepped onto the porch, led the way to the garage and unlocked the side door. They entered and Barton flipped the light switch. "There it is."

Luke stared at it. Was this the car used to kidnap the women and return with their bodies? "May I see the back seat and trunk?"

Mr. Barton narrowed his eyes and shrugged. He pushed a button on his key fob and the trunk popped open. He pushed again and the locks clicked. At the back of the car, Luke lifted the trunk lid and directed his flashlight all around.

Barton leaned a hip against the side of the trunk and

crossed his arms. "What are you looking for, detective?"

"Does anyone else use this car?"

Barton frowned and lowered his arms. "My son does occasionally when his is in the shop."

"What's his name?"

"What's this about?"

"Someone committed a crime with a car similar to this one. I'm just trying to rule out as many as I can. So, what's your son's name?"

He raised his voice. "My son wouldn't have done anything illegal."

"Then there's no problem telling me his name." Luke could get it easy enough without Barton's cooperation.

Barton sighed. "Alex Barton."

Blood wouldn't be visible on the black carpet. Luke pulled out a roll of masking tape and tore off a piece. He rolled the tape over several spots. He inspected it. Not a scientific way to search for evidence, but he didn't see any hair on it. He checked the back seat, and found nothing there either. If he had found red hair, it wouldn't be admissible, but he would likely have a more concrete suspect to pursue.

"When was the last time your son borrowed your car?"

"About a month ago. Hey, is this about that serial killer case?" A touch of surprise entered his voice. "Don't those guys have lunatic parents? Which my son does not."

"Everything's good here, Mr. Barton. I'd appreciate it if you didn't mention this to anyone. Thanks for your time." Luke hated when the person he was questioning figured out what it was about.

When Luke got back into his car he wrote up his notes. It wasn't likely this car was used to kidnap the women, but he'd check out Alex Barton's driver's license picture, and talk to him anyway. His father would've become suspicious if he'd borrowed it too many times. He could have alternated with his own, unless it was too distinctive.

The fourth house was the last one inside the city limits. No one was home but the car sat in the driveway. The back seat was piled with papers, a briefcase and a wadded up fast-food bag. Someone who took his time cleaning the bodies of his victims probably had a neater car than this.

He added more notes to the list and checked his watch. He'd have time for one more visit before picking up Sherry.

He pulled out his phone. "Hi, Mom. Can I drop Sherry off with you after I pick her up? I need to do some calls after dinner."

"That's fine, Luke. Why don't you stay for dinner? I can have it ready when you get here."

"Sounds good. Thanks, Mom." Besides Shannon, his mom was the person he missed while he was away.

Luke drove fifteen minutes to the next address on his list. He pulled into the driveway of a mansion. The two-story building was at least a hundred feet long. Arborvitae bordered the property, and a seven- or eight-foot white privacy fence joined the bushes to the house.

A pretty redhead leaned into a white Lexus and stood up with a briefcase in her hand.

Luke got out and walked to the back of her car. "Susan Jeffers? I'm Detective Luke Cade." He showed his badge.

She frowned. "Detective?"

"Yes. I'm investigating a crime that involved a dark colored car." He scanned his list. "I see that you have a dark gray Lexus registered to you."

"Yes, it's in my name, but it's my husband's car. What kind of crime?"

"Right now, I'm just trying to cross cars off my list. Is your husband's car here now?"

"No, he's still at work for another hour or so."

"Where does he work?"

"He's a golf pro at Willow Ridge Golf Club."

It was a pretty exclusive club. Luke didn't golf, but the guys he worked with used the public course.

"What's his name?"

She put one hand on her hip and stared at him.

"I'm just trying to whittle down my list, Mrs. Jeffers. It could be none of these are the car I'm looking for. I don't have complete information on it." He was pretty sure that if he waited long enough, acting expectant, she'd talk.

"His name is Brian Jeffers."

"Thank you, Mrs. Jeffers." Luke nodded, returned to his car and checked his watch. Willow Ridge was just a short distance out of his way. He should have time to stop. He hoped Susan Jeffers waited for her husband to get home before telling him about Luke's visit.

Five minutes later, Luke turned at the Willow Ridge sign, tan background with gold lettering, surrounded by low, flowering bushes. He found a parking space beside a dark gray Lexus. He checked his list against the plate number. Since it was a match, he donned the tape again. If he got the chance, he'd check it. He climbed out of the car, and curled his fingers into his palm, then carefully slipped it into his jacket pocket. He leaned down to the back window of the Lexus and shielded the sun with his right hand. The back seat area was spotless.

"What are you doing?" an irritated male voice asked.

Luke straightened, and scrutinized a man standing at the front corner of the car. Dark hair, not quite to the collar, clean shaven, prominent chin, and average height and weight. "Are you Brian Jeffers?"

"Who wants to know?" The man's lips tightened into a straight line, and he crossed his arms over his chest.

"I'm Detective Luke Cade." He flipped open his badge. "And you are?"

The man glared at Luke. "Brian Jeffers. Why are you looking into my car?"

"It matches the description of a car I'm looking for, so I'm trying to eliminate some." Maybe if he didn't mention the list, Jeffers wouldn't feel as threatened. Luke gestured toward the car. "Do you mind if I look inside?" Luke gave him a slight smile, trying to disarm him.

"I don't have to show you without a warrant." Jeffers slipped his hands into his pockets.

"That's true, but it's no big deal, is it?"

They stared at each other for several seconds. Luke was determined he wouldn't be the first to break.

"Fine," Jeffers sighed. He pulled out his keys, and the car beeped twice. "Have at it."

Luke opened the back door and leaned in, running the tape around the floor and along the crack between the seat and the back. He made sure to block Jeffers seeing what he was doing. He slipped his hand back into his pocket, stood and closed the door. "How about the trunk?"

Jeffers lips tightened again, but he beeped his fob and the trunk lid popped open a couple inches.

Luke lifted the lid, hoping Jeffers stayed where he was so he wouldn't see Luke in the trunk. A pair of work gloves sat on the right beside a set of neatly wound jumper cables and a beach blanket. He ran the tape around the bottom and into some of the corners of the trunk and straightened, slipping his hand back into his pocket and closed the trunk. Jeffers had remained where he was.

"Thanks, Mr. Jeffers." Luke walked around the back of his own car.

"That's it?" Jeffers asked.

"That's it." Luke cocked his head. "Should there be more?"

Jeffers shook his head. "No. Of course not."

Luke drove one handed to the club entrance and stopped. From the glove box, he extracted an evidence bag, and slipped the tape inside and labeled it. Red hairs clung to the tape.

Of course, Jeffers' wife had red hair, and they could have been picked up in the backseat or the trunk. Hopefully, his team could match them to one of the victims.

Chapter 11

Thursday morning, as Luke passed Gary's desk, he gestured him. "Come to my office. We need to talk." He'd spent two more days visiting every car owner on the list Gary had given him, as well as an evening canvassing the neighborhood near the beach. He sat behind his desk, pulled the list from his pocket, and dropped it in front of him.

"I've got one guy I want you to check out."

"Sure thing." Gary leaned forward. "Which one?"

"Allen Smith. He was extremely nervous when I talked to him."

Gary tapped his knee. "Okay. I've got one, too. Reggie Faulkner. He was a bit too belligerent. I'll check police records, find out their work hours and talk to their co-workers. Maybe find out what these two do on their time off."

"Don't forget to check if they're on your key list."

"That, too." Gary stood, a gleam in his eyes. Luke had learned Gary loved digging up dirt on suspected criminals. "I'm on it. I'll keep you posted."

Luke nodded and stared at his list. "I'll check out Brian Jeffers myself." As Gary exited, Luke booted up his computer and picked up the phone. "Hey, Dave. It's Luke. Have you got anything for me on those hair samples?"

"How are you, Luke? I'm doing great."

"Sorry. I'm so focused on this case, most of the time I don't think of anything else." Except for Shannon, and getting this bastard before he had another chance to get his nasty hands on her.

"I'll let you off the hook this time. Anyway, four of the strands of hair don't match any of the victims. The other three need more analysis. Give me another day, and I'll email you a report."

"All right. Thanks." Even if the hairs didn't match the victims, it didn't mean the car owner could be ruled out.

First up with Jeffers was to check his police record. All he found were two speeding tickets four years before. He'd also been cited for defective equipment with the second ticket. The nine-year-old vehicle was quite a contrast to what he currently drove. Maybe a golf pro made more money than Luke thought.

The message icon appeared on Luke's screen, and he clicked on his email. The message from Dave listed each of the samples that didn't have red hair. One sample was from Allen Smith's car from Gary's list.

He checked his watch. Time to get to Willow Ridge Golf Club.

Jeffers' car was absent from the lot. A couple of middle-aged men headed toward cars, with golf bags over their shoulders. They must have gotten in a round before work. A golf cart caught his eye as it stopped at a distant green. Everything about the club screamed money. Luscious green grass, bushes perfectly pruned, a fountain in the middle of the nearest pond, and a beautiful large building. A sign gave directions to a restaurant, bar, event room, and membership.

Luke followed the arrow to membership, figuring it would lead to an office with a manager. Voices drew him to a half open door. He nudged it open, and tapped on the door frame. He introduced himself to the woman and man seated at desks, and flashed his badge. The woman's eyebrows rose and the man leaned back in his chair.

"I'd like to get some information on Brian Jeffers."

"What do you want to know?" the man asked.

Luke stepped closer. "Who are you?"

"I'm Trevor Bailey, the owner."

"Mr. Bailey, can you tell me how long Jeffers has worked here?"

"Nearly five years. Why?"

"Just gathering background information for a case we're working on. He may have been in contact with someone we should talk to. What days does he work?"

Bailey stared at him, maybe trying to coax Luke into giving more information. Without taking his eyes from Luke, he spoke. "Marcy, pull up Brian's schedule."

She clicked keys on her keyboard. "Tuesday, Thursday, Friday and every other Saturday."

Wednesdays worked for three of the victims. "What are his hours?"

"Nine to six. Except Fridays when he leaves at three."

Two victims had gone missing late in the day on Fridays. "Has he come in late or left early?"

Bailey shrugged. "Marcy?"

"He's been late a few times, but not when he has a student. I don't think he's a morning person."

"Can you tell me which days?"

She shook her head. "No. It's never been more than a half-hour, usually only a few minutes."

Damn. That could have been helpful for Shannon and Carrie Lawson's cases, since they were both attacked on mornings that Jeffers worked.

"What about leaving early?"

"Sometimes he does when his last student of the day cancels."

Luke stepped closer to Marcy. "Do you keep track of that?"

"I keep track of the cancellations so we can credit the fee to the next lesson. But Brian doesn't always leave, and I can't remember which days he did."

Maybe they were getting somewhere. "Can I get a list of the days he had cancellations for the past three months?"

She frowned. "But he might not have left."

"I can sort through that later."

"All right." She folded back the page of a lined pad of paper, glanced at the monitor and wrote four dates. Another click gave her one more date. She tore off the page and handed it to Luke.

"Thank you." He glanced between the two. "Does he get along with everybody?"

Trevor answered. "Yeah, everybody likes him. The members like him, too."

"He's married, isn't he?"

"Yeah, his wife's a member. That's how they met. Had a nice wedding right here at the club."

"Oh, when was that?" If they'd met here then they hadn't been married long.

Bailey glanced at the woman. "It's been about two years, hasn't it, Marcy?"

"Two and a half." Her gaze went to the wall with two rows of pictures.

Wedding photos. He stepped closer and found the picture with Susan and Brian Jeffers. She was a beautiful bride. The date was just as Marcy had said.

Maybe his and Shannon's picture would end up on the wall here. But he was getting way ahead of anything he'd had with her so far.

"Well, thank you for your time." He nodded to them and ignored their puzzled expressions. Luke climbed into his car as Jeffers arrived. He'd get an earful from his co-workers, but it couldn't be helped.

On the drive back to the station, he reviewed the new information. None of it offered Jeffers an alibi for any of the murders, which didn't mean he was guilty, but left him as a good suspect.

At his desk, Luke searched the local newspaper's website on Brian Jeffers. He found articles about golf tournaments Jeffers had managed, and a society page article with pictures of his wedding. It said that Susan Argyle was the widow of Anthony Argyle, Jr. He searched the Argyle name and found several articles. The man had owned AAJ Electronics, had two sons and a daughter, and Susan was his second wife. The sons, Theodore and Bradley, worked at AAJ. Luke calculated that Anthony and Susan's daughter, Autumn, was now eight.

Luke opened the probate court website and searched for Anthony Argyle's will. All of his property was divided equally between his three children. His wife would receive an allowance and was allowed to live in the family home until her death. He wondered if Jeffers knew when he married Susan that she didn't inherit.

He leaned back and laced his fingers behind his head. The name Argyle seemed familiar, but he couldn't place it. He'd heard it recently. He closed his eyes, and worked at suppressing all his jumbled thoughts. The technique helped on many other occasions to extract a piece of elusive information.

Images of Shannon intruded, and he forced himself to ignore them as well. It could have been seconds or minutes, but he remembered the name Argyle from the beach padlock key list. Bradley Argyle had been a lifeguard in his teens.

Either they had another suspect or Jeffers had stolen the key from Bradley. Bradley's car wasn't on their car registration list, although, he could have used Jeffers car. Two suspects with the same redhead in their lives. His money was still on Jeffers, especially since the man's appearance matched the homeless man's description, but he needed to follow all leads. Maybe Bradley resented his father's much younger wife.

Chapter 12

Shannon's heart leaped when she stepped out her door, and she frowned. The last two times she'd run with Luke, she'd totally ignored him like she'd done at first. She started running without speaking to him.

Every time her brain was idle, she'd catch herself going over what he'd told her. After three days, she'd gotten past the worst of the hurt and anger of Luke leaving her for Annie. Once, she'd been able to think about his story, it really sunk in that Luke hadn't had sex since he left her. Well, maybe. She'd found it hard to believe when he told her, but now she teetered on the fence. He'd said Annie was too sick when they got married, and by the time she was well, they'd already established their relationship.

Remembering how she and Luke had been together, she found it hard to believe he'd forgo sex. Once their relationship progressed to that point, nearly every time they got together, they ended up in bed.

And he was too decent to have dated other women while he was married. At least the Luke she used to know. But the Luke she thought she knew wouldn't have left her the way he did. It was too hard to figure out who the real Luke was.

All the time Annie was sick, Luke would have pretty much been a single parent with another person to care for as well. Shannon couldn't imagine trying to do that. He'd had a few hard years. Of his own making—but hard, none-the-less.

And now he had to take care of his daughter and put great deal of effort into finding this serial killer.

"Luke?" She let him catch up to her. She glanced at him, then back to the path ahead. It was easier to speak without looking at him. "Why didn't you make love to your wife?" She took a quick peek as his eyes widened. Yeah, she'd surprised herself with that question, too.

He grabbed her arm, and swung around in front of her, halting her. He took her other arm.

She cocked her head, a little bit afraid to hear his reply. She closed her eyes, listening to their quickened breaths, almost wishing she hadn't asked the question.

"Shannon?" He didn't say anything more until she opened her eyes again. "I didn't feel that way about her. The only woman I wanted to make love with was you. I still feel that way. I love you. I know you have every reason not to trust me, but I'm not going to stop trying to earn your love back."

He dropped his arms, and she continued to stare into his eyes. He seemed sincere, but could she believe him? Could she trust him again?

He ran, for the first time ahead of her. She hurried to catch up.

~~~

Luke was elated that she had actually asked him a question about Annie. It was a sign that she'd listened to him this time and had been thinking about it. He hoped it helped her to understand he still had feelings for her.

Shannon caught up and ran beside him, surprising him that she hadn't run past.

This was one small step. He was still a long way from gaining her trust. Even if she believed what he'd told her about his life with Annie, she might not believe that he loved her enough. And maybe it didn't matter. She believed he loved her before, and he left. What he needed to do was make her understand he wouldn't leave her again, but he didn't know how to do that.

They finished the run in silence. Luke waited on the sidewalk as Shannon entered her house, then ran another loop.

Now that he'd cleared the air about Annie, he was ready to talk to Shannon about everyday things. They used to have long, fun conversations. Maybe if he eased her into that, she'd feel comfortable with him again and would see he wasn't the same person he used to be.

He had so much to tell her about Sherry, his mom, and work. Maybe if he opened up, she would, too. He wasn't much for monologues, but if that's what it took to get a conversation going, he'd do it.

It wouldn't be easy to keep talking while running, but easier than the first few times he ran with Shannon. It was the only time he had a chance to make amends, so he didn't have a choice.

He used to run often, but he'd slacked off. Between taking care of Sherry, and Annie when she was sick, and extra hours for work, there'd been no time. Now, he enjoyed getting back to his old routine. Especially since Shannon used to be his running partner.

With that decided, he increased his pace. His legs were like rubber by the time he returned to his car.

~~~

The water was cool on her heated skin as it flowed through Shannon's hair and ran down her face. Her body warmed as she remembered running behind Luke after the sex question. She'd enjoyed watching his legs pump, his shoulders bunch as his arms swung, and that tight butt. She flushed with memories of running her hands over his body. He had more muscles now than the last time she'd touched him. His chest was broader, his arms thicker. Maybe he lifted weights. Or it was because he was older. Would his body feel harder?

A part of her was awakening, and she wished it'd go back to sleep. Luke became more tempting every time she saw him. His body strong as he kept watch over her. Almost all the time they'd spent together had been while running. She could imagine the heavy breathing having a different cause.

She growled, not wanting to think about him like that. Thoughts of being intimate with anyone had been expunged from her mind years ago. She couldn't think about Luke that way because it would bring her one step closer to giving in to him. And she wouldn't survive if he left again.

Chapter 13

An email message waited for Luke when he turned on his computer. Dave's analysis was complete. None of the hair samples matched the victims. One had red hair, but that was from Jeffers' car and his wife was a redhead. He leaned back in his chair and sighed, picked up a pencil and tapped the eraser on the desk. He still had a gut feeling that the killer was Jeffers, but there wasn't proof. Not having an alibi wasn't good enough. He had to dig deeper and keep an eye on Jeffers.

All the abductions would likely have occurred while Jeffers' wife was working. He couldn't take the women to his home, so where would he go? He searched county records and found that the Argyle family owned three properties, the house they lived in, the manufacturing plant and a house on Orchid Lake.

Thursday was a work day for Jeffers, so he'd be at the golf course soon.

Luke would leave to check out the lake house in an hour. He wouldn't be able to get in without probable cause and a warrant, but he could check the outside and talk to the neighbors.

It was over an hour drive, with light traffic for the first ten minutes and few cars after that. He took the turnoff for Orchid Lake Road. The first two houses were small, old cabins. They'd probably been in the families for years or someone would have torn them down and built new by now. The next few houses on the lake side were large, well maintained and appeared to be less than twenty years old. Not all the houses had mailboxes on the street, so he figured the ones without were vacation homes.

He checked addresses on the mailboxes. Almost there. The next house didn't have a box, and the one after that, the number was higher than the one he searched for. Luke parked on the road and walked back. He spotted the house number beside the door. This was the Argyle property. The log home, definitely not a cabin, sat closer to the lake than to the road, and the land gradually descended to the water. The two-story second home was bigger than the homes his family and friends owned.

He strode up a cement walk from the driveway to the front steps and ascended the four treads. He crossed the twelve-foot porch that spanned the front of the house, and peeked into the windows gracing both sides of the door.

Along the side of the house, he noted two basement windows. If Jeffers was the killer, and used this house, then he probably took the women to the basement. He squatted beside a window and shielded his eyes with his hands, but wasn't able to see anything in the darkness. He did the same at the second window with the same result.

At the back of the home, a three seasons porch ran half the length of the house. Most of its windows were open. A dining area was closest to him and the other end held a cozy living room arrangement. A fireplace set with wood, faced the couch. It was more like an expensive luxury retreat than a porch. His mother's screened porch held wicker furniture.

A dock with a power boat and two jet skis extended from the sandy beach. A small building stood at the edge of the water. Luke headed for it and peered in the window. Light shown through the window on the far side, revealing life jackets, paddles, beach chairs and toys. This would also be a good place to hide the women.

Back at the road, Luke scanned both directions. The area was wooded between houses, so only the house directly across had a view of the property. A silver Rav4 in the drive hopefully meant someone was home. He strode the brick walk, and climbed the steps. The door opened as he reached it. A nosy neighbor could be a big help. The woman stared through the screen and waited for him to speak.

"Hi, I'm Detective Luke Cade." He displayed his badge. "And what's your name, please?"

"Paige Wallace. Is there something wrong, detective?"

"I'm working on a case, and wondered if you could help."

The woman tipped her head. Equal amounts of gray threaded through her short, curly brown hair. He stood one step below her, their eyes almost level. Her wiry frame seemed full of energy as Paige twisted the doorknob back and forth.

He half turned and pointed to the log house. "Have you seen any unusual activity across the street in the past few months?"

Her eyebrows rose. "Why don't you come inside and have a seat?"

"Thank you." He followed her into a living room. It seemed she might have a lot to tell him.

He scanned the room. An overstuffed couch with a coffee table faced a wide screen TV with a DVD player beneath. It'd been a while since he saw one of those. Two matching chairs sat on opposite walls from each other. He stepped in front of the picture window, staring out at the Argyle house across the street. There was a view of the front of the house, the right side yard, and the water and dock.

She spoke to his back. "Would you like ice tea or water?"

"No, thanks."

She sat on the couch, so he sat in the closest chair, and rested his elbows on his thighs.

"Have you seen activity in the last few months?"

"What kind of activity?"

"Cars coming, maybe not staying long. Anything that you found strange."

She squinted towards the house. "There were a couple of times," she spoke slowly, "when the dark gray car pulled up beside the screen porch. Usually, they all park in front."

Maybe the driver didn't want to be seen. "Had you seen the car before?"

She drummed her fingers on the couch arm. "That car's been there a number of times. Months ago, Susan and her daughter, and I assume her husband arrived in it. She never introduced him to us."

"So, you know Susan Jeffers."

"I know her as Susan Argyle."

"When was the last time you saw Susan?"

Mrs. Wallace pursed her lips. "Sometime last fall. She used to come once or twice a month with her first husband, Anthony, and the rest of the family. Then after he died, she brought her daughter once in a while, and sometimes one or both of the sons came."

"What about the new husband?"

She clenched her hands. "He came with her a couple of times."

"But lately, it's been just him?"

She shook her head and scowled. "No. The first time he came without his wife he brought a woman. He had to help her out of the backseat since she was staggering drunk."

Backseat. Why not in the front? Luke's heart kicked up. She might have been a drugged victim. "Did you recognize the woman?"

She shook her head. "The woman's hair was red, but not

the same shade as Susan's."

He leaned forward. "What did you think of that?"

She grimaced. "I feel so bad for Susan. She doesn't deserve to have a husband who cheats on her. She and Anthony were so much in love. You could see it when we had cookouts with them. People talked about the huge age difference between them, but you only had to see them together to know how much they meant to each other. We haven't had any get-togethers since she remarried."

Not pertinent to his case, so he had to get her back on track. Sometimes, when he let a witness run-on, it revealed surprising information. "You mentioned another time when the car pulled to the back."

She nodded. "And it was worse that time."

Luke widened his eyes. "How's that?"

"She was so drunk that he had to carry her."

Or unconscious. "Do you think it was the same woman?"

She stared through the window as if in thought. "Probably not. The second one had bright red, almost orange hair." Anger stirred in her eyes.

If the man was having affairs or hook-ups, he wasn't likely to go for just redheads. "Would you know the dates of these two incidents?"

"Not the first one. I just happened to look out the window. But the second time…I was going out." She closed her eyes. This might be their big break.

"Ah, I was meeting my husband and friends for a late dinner. Hold on while I check my calendar."

Luke drew a deep breath as the woman hurried from the room. He vibrated with excitement that they might be closing in.

Mrs. Wallace returned a few moments later with a wall calendar. She sat in the same spot, set the calendar on the coffee table and flipped pages. Luke leaned closer and waited.

Triumphantly, she pointed. "There it is." She turned the calendar towards him. In the square was written *Dinner with Jack and Fran.*

Luke's chest tightened. It was the same day Jordan Ford had gone missing, and she had orange-red hair. Had he found the killer? Or at least the location of the murders?

"Mrs. Wallace, can I get your phone number before I leave?" He noted it. "Here's my card. Call me if you think of anything else, or if you see more strange activity across the road."

He strode back to his car with a lighter step. If he was a kid, he'd jump up and down, and chuckled at Mrs. Wallace's reaction if she saw him do it.

He made notes of all she'd told him, then stopped for lunch on his way back to the station.

Luke paused at Gary's desk, but the detective was on the phone. Luke pointed toward his office, and Gary nodded.

He'd only gotten his suspect document open when Gary strode in and dropped into the chair in front of the desk.

Gary started right in. "Allen Smith is out. He was clear across the country on business for two of the murders. I'm still checking into Reggie Faulkner. All I've got is that he has no alibi for any of the kidnappings. His only brushes with the law are a speeding ticket and two parking tickets."

"My number one is Brian Jeffers," Luke said. He lifted his hand and held up one finger. "He has Wednesdays off and gets out early on Fridays." He lifted a second finger. "His wife's family owns a house on Orchid Lake. A neighbor saw him bring two women to the house that appeared drunk. He carried in the second woman the night Jordan Ford disappeared, and she had bright orange hair. And, his wife is…a redhead."

Gary whistled. "She's got red hair?"

"Maybe he's doing to these women what he wants to do to his wife. I think he married her because he thought she was rich. Her rich husband died. Jeffers likely assumed she inherited a boatload of money. If he killed her after they were married a while, then he'd inherit...well, along with her daughter. But it turns out she didn't inherit anything when her first husband died. She gets an allowance and can live in the house as long as she wants. Her daughter and her husband's sons inherited everything. So, Jeffers is enjoying living the rich life, but he can't get it for himself. He's trapped."

Gary slapped his leg. "He sounds like a real possibility. What do you want to do now?"

"Let's concentrate on Jeffers. I'm going to bring him in for questioning, find out if he has alibis. Why don't you dig into his past? Get his work history and talk to old girlfriends."

Gary stood. "I'm on it." He walked out the door.

Luke leaned back in his chair. He steepled his fingers in front of his mouth and tapped his index fingers against his lips. He had to do this right. Jeffers should arrive home early on Friday, and Luke would be waiting to take him to the station. He'd make sure to be done in time for Jeffers to be back before his wife got home from work. No need to involve her yet.

One step closer to keeping Shannon safe. No case had ever been as important to him as this one. Getting the killer off the streets not only saved other women's lives, but the woman he loved.

Chapter 14

Luke finished typing, and glanced up as Gary dropped into the chair in front of Luke's desk. Over Gary's shoulder, he watched the buzz in the main office area. A laugh from one of the guys caught his attention. He hadn't gotten back into that kind of camaraderie yet. Between getting his daughter settled into her new life, trying to get Shannon to trust him, and keeping her safe by catching this serial killer, he hadn't had time.

He glanced at Gary. "Do you have something for me?"

"Yeah. Jeffers last job was at a golf club in Chicago for nearly two years. They got rid of him because he kept hitting on the single women. The women were getting annoyed and started to complain. Before that, he hopped around from club to club, not staying for much more than a year at each. Probably worked his way unsuccessfully through the women. Maybe he was trying to find a rich wife."

"Maybe. Then he gets here and finds a lonely, apparently rich widow." Luke nodded, disliking the guy more with everything they found out about him. "Good work. Anything else?"

"I'm still looking for any girlfriends, but he may have just concentrated on the golf women."

"Okay, thanks, Gary." He checked his watch. "I'm leaving shortly to bring Jeffers in for questioning. Your info might help."

Gary nodded and headed for the door.

Luke threw down his pen, left the building and drove to

the Jeffers' home, parking on the street.

He tapped his fingers on the steering wheel, waiting for the man to arrive. No cars sat in the driveway, but he didn't know about the garages. Two double doors meant there could be four cars inside. He scanned the building. Four people lived in that monster of a house. From his vantage point on the street, he noticed the house extended well beyond where the garage attached to the side. The mansion had a wing.

And Jeffers likely thought it would all be his once he married Susan Argyle. Instead, they were practically renting.

Minutes later, a car turned in and parked near the house. Luke jumped out of his car, and marched up to Jeffers.

"Brian Jeffers, I need to ask you some questions."

Jeffers kept the door between them, and dropped his arm across the top of it. His face showed no emotion. "Oh?"

"You'll have to come down to the station with me."

"I don't want to go to the station. Talk here." His other hand gripped the door, white knuckled.

"Afraid not. Do you really want your wife to come home while we're talking? I'll try to have you back before she gets home."

Jeffers sighed. "Fine. I'll follow you there."

Luke tried to read him but couldn't. Jeffers wouldn't likely run. The money was too easy staying in the Argyle household. He probably figured he was one of many being interviewed, and that he was too smart for the police.

Luke nodded. "All right."

Luke strode to his car as Jeffers got back into his, and waited for Jeffers to back into the street, then led the way to the station. His eyes strayed to his rearview mirror as much as the road ahead of him.

They parked and Luke took Jeffers to an interrogation room.

Luke pointed at a chair. "Have a seat. Do you want a

drink?"

Jeffers shook his head.

"I'll be back in a minute." Luke headed into the main office area and called out to Gary. "I've got him. Do you want to watch?"

"Yeah."

Luke stopped in front of a vending machine and bought two bottles of water. He opened and gulped down half of one, then capped it. The other, he wiped off with a paper towel and carried it by its top. His gut told him that Jeffers was likely the man who'd tried to abduct Shannon. Who'd killed Jane Roslin and six other women. What he wanted to do was choke a confession out of the man, but everything that happened in the interview room was taped, so that wouldn't happen.

He took a deep breath, rolled his shoulders, and went back to the room with Jeffers. He set the bottles on the table and dropped into the chair opposite him. He picked up his bottle and took a drink as he stared Jeffers down, then read the man his rights.

"Understand?" Luke wondered if Jeffers had been in a situation before to require hearing his rights.

"Yes."

Luke's back was to the two-way mirror that Gary stood behind. Maybe other interested officers had joined him. Luke glanced at the clock on the wall in front of him. He still had almost two hours before Susan Jeffers arrived home. Sunlight slanted through the one window, lighting a rectangle on the floor with bars passing through it.

Luke leaned back, trying to convey that the interview didn't matter as much as it did. He might as well start with a question that might make Jeffers think he had an out. "Does anyone else drive your car?"

"I suppose my mechanic does." The corners of Jeffers'

mouth turned up into a small smile, toying with Luke.

There were no nervous twitches, or fidgeting feet, as if he had nothing to fear from Luke's questions. Even most innocent people Luke talked to were slightly nervous.

The remote possibility that Bradley Argyle had used Jeffers car to kill the women was gone. "Is it in the shop much?"

Jeffers shrugged. "Every couple of months."

"I guess I won't buy a Lexus. Can you give me dates?"

Jeffers tipped his palm up and smirked. "Sorry, I don't have my calendar."

"Don't you have one on your phone?"

"You know, I do have some dates on my phone. May I?" He pointed toward his pocket. Luke tipped his head in a nod. Jeffers pulled out his phone and his fingers swiped and touched, then he said, "June fifteenth and sixteenth. April twenty-second and twenty-third. I'm not sure before that."

Angie Harris and Shannon. Luke had the dates memorized. He'd have to check his notes to find out if a car was seen during those times. It couldn't be a coincidence that during two incidents Jeffers' car was supposedly in the shop. He'd likely used the shop loaner while his had work done. Or he could have driven his wife to work and used her car.

"What shop did you use?"

"It was the dealership on Main Street."

"So, during those times you didn't have a car?"

"Actually, they gave me a loaner." Jeffers crossed his arms on his chest and smirked.

Jeffers could drive a different car and not have a rental record. It was perfect.

"While you've got your calendar out, can you tell me what you did after you left work on May fifteenth?"

Jeffers swiped across his phone. "I met up with some friends for drinks about seven."

"What about before that?"

Jeffers shrugged. "Nothing here. I must have gone home."

"What about the morning of Friday, June seventeenth?"

He shook his head without checking his calendar. "I barely make it out the door to get to work on time. I'm not going to do anything before that."

Luke had already found out there would be no record of Jeffers arriving late for work. It was interesting that Jeffers assumed Luke meant before work, when it could have been any time in the morning. "And the evening of Friday, June nineteenth?"

Jeffers referred to his phone. "My wife and I went to a play."

"What time did it start?"

"Eight o'clock."

Jeffers could have had just enough time to kidnap Jordan Ford, take her to the lake house and return home. Then return later to finish her off.

"Where were you the early evening of July seventeenth?"

Jeffers put his palms flat on the table. "What's all this about?" Finally, a reaction to the date requests, but still no fear in his eyes. Just an average Joe, curious about the questions. Although, most Joe's would be worried that they could be arrested for something they didn't do.

Luke narrowed his eyes. "I'm just trying to fill in my calendar. You're one of several people who own a dark colored Lexus that we're talking to." Luke was sure Jeffers knew what this was about. On the slight chance that he wasn't the killer, Luke didn't want to scare him.

"So, July seventeenth?" Luke raised an eyebrow.

Jeffers looked down at his calendar and swiped once. "Nothing listed, so I must have been home." He kept a neutral expression.

Luke stood. "That's it for now. Let me show you out." He opened the door and pointed. "Down the hall and straight through the desks."

Luke hurried to his office, and Gary joined him, sitting in front of the desk. Tried to gauge Gary's reaction.

"You didn't ask him about all the dates."

"There'll be plenty of time for that later. I wanted to get a feel for his responses." Luke grinned. "He has no alibi. Even his two attempts didn't cover the time they needed to."

"So, what now?"

"Now we watch him. It's been three weeks since the last killing. He'll strike again in the next one to two weeks. We'll try to catch him in the act of kidnapping someone."

Gary nodded.

"I want you to put together a detail. Follow him to work. Be there when he leaves. Find out what he does on his days off. Add me to your rotation, but not early mornings when I run with Shannon." He slid his keyboard closer. "In the meantime, I'm going to put together everything we know and try to get a warrant to search Jeffers' car and the Argyle lake house."

The car likely wouldn't yield much, but if the murders occurred at the lake house, there should be evidence Jeffers had missed.

Chapter 15

Shannon stepped out her door, and Luke straightened up from leaning on the railing post. "Morning, Shannon." After he said it, he realized that he'd never greeted her when they started a run. He'd said he was running with her or some related comment, but mostly he said nothing. He was like a silent sentinel, following her. How had he never noticed? He couldn't gain her trust if he didn't speak with her.

Shannon glanced at him and stretched her legs. Without checking that Luke followed, she started her run. He quickened his pace and fell in beside her.

"I've been slowly reconnecting with my old friends," he told her. "It's been more difficult than I expected." His oldest friends were Will's, too, so he understood that. Fellow officers that he'd known before were more accepting of his return.

She glanced toward him, her lips thinned.

"I think some of the guys think they're being disloyal to Will if we resume our friendship."

"I'm sure it will work out eventually. Or, gee, make new friends."

It was a bit sarcastic, but she'd given a response to something he'd said. Maybe he'd get through to her after all.

"Sherry and Willa are becoming friends. I think they could become as close as Will and I once were." He still missed Will's friendship. They'd known each other since kindergarten, just like Sherry and Willa. That was a lot of years of friendship to throw away. At least, he now understood why Will hated him.

"I'm glad Sherry's found Willa. Willa's a sweet little girl. She could use a good friend after what she's been through."

Luke's stomach churned. What else could have hurt this family? He hadn't heard of anything. Surely, his mother would have told him if it was serious.

"What has she been through?"

Shannon glanced his way, sadness in her eyes. "About a year ago, Leah was in an accident. A teenager, fleeing from police, ran a red light and t-boned her car. She spent months in the hospital. They didn't know if she'd walk again. Then she spent months in rehab. Through all that, Willa didn't get as much attention as she really needed. I did what I could. I spent a lot of time over there while Will was at the hospital with Leah. I read Willa stories, tucked her in at night, took her to the park."

He wondered if caring for Willa, doing the things a mother would do, soothed Shannon after her loss, or made it worse because she wasn't doing those things for her own child.

"That must have been hard for all of them. How's Leah now?" In some ways Willa experienced what Sherry had. Her mother being at a hospital all that time, seeing her mother in pain when she was home.

"She still has a ways to go. She has a limp, but refuses to use a cane now. She tires quickly if she has to walk far, but she's getting there."

He wished he could have given his friend support. It must have been tough for Will to see two women he loved almost die and go through what they did. Luke knew that Annie's suffering would lead to death. Was it worse to not know which way it would go?

"I had the advantage, if you could call it that, to plan out ahead of time how to take care of Sherry. We spent time together, and I rarely missed tucking her in. I tried to make up for her mother not being there."

Luke was surprised when they crossed the street and were almost back to Shannon's house. It took longer to speak because they were running, but the time had passed too quickly.

He ran up to the door with her, and took her arm, turning her towards him.

"Thanks for talking with me, Shannon."

With his other hand, he lifted her chin. He hoped to catch her by surprise. He kissed her. His plan was to give her a quick kiss, but once his lips touched hers, he wanted so much more. He released her arm and slipped his hand to her back and pulled her closer.

He'd finally found his oasis after being lost in the desert. He only realized she hadn't been responding when her hands slid up his chest and her tongue barely touched his. She sighed as her hands continued upward and wove through his hair.

He feathered kisses across her cheek to her ear and nibbled the lobe. "I have to go," he whispered.

Shannon stiffened. She tore herself away, eyes widened as she bumped the door, then shoved him. He caught the railing to stop from tumbling down the stairs. She turned her back, fumbled with her keys until she got the door unlocked and opened, then slipped inside without speaking.

Luke rested his hand on the door jam and leaned against it. Progress, but not enough. Shannon's heart had forgiven him, but he still needed to reach her mind.

~~~

After locking the door, Shannon raced to the bathroom and turned on the shower. As she jerked off her clothes, she chastised herself. She couldn't believe that she'd allowed Luke to kiss her. Then when she was going to push him away, her hands decided they liked the feel of his chest and needed to explore. He definitely had bigger muscles than the last time she'd touched him. Her lips had betrayed her, too.

"Grrr. Stop it!" She stepped into the spray and yelped from the cold. It still wasn't cooling her physical need for Luke. What was he doing to her? She didn't want to feel anything for him. She was afraid to trust him with her heart again, but her thoughts kept strayed to him. Like now.

Too often lately, she'd recall memories of the good times they had together—the feelings she had for him, and the love in his eyes.

Lying eyes.

But if he didn't love her, never had, then why would he come back? Why try so hard to convince her he cared? Any number of women would gladly soothe the grieving widower, and they'd be a whole lot easier to date than her.

She needed to think about anything but Luke. Work. She had a good routine that pulled her through so much turmoil. Work wasn't stress free, but it didn't affect her heart. She had two new patients and needed to review their massage plans. That was what she'd concentrate on.

Chapter 16

Luke leaned back in his chair and read the last report. Over two weeks of following Jeffers yielded nothing but bored detectives. He hadn't done anything suspicious, but there also had been no bodies found. Footsteps echoed in his office, and he glanced up.

Gary scowled and dropped into a chair. "Jason Connors lost Jeffers last night."

"How did that happen?" These were well trained men. There shouldn't have been a slip up.

"Jeffers went into the mall. He didn't come back out."

"How long did Connors wait?"

"He called me after three hours. I told him to go to Jeffers house."

"So, Jeffers left by a different door and had another car waiting. You should have called me last night. What time did they arrive at the mall and was Jeffers home when Connors arrived?"

"They got to the mall at five-oh-five. Connors got to Jeffers' home at eight-twenty and Jeffers arrived home at ten-sixteen."

"Was Jeffers in his own car?"

Gary nodded.

"You should have kept Connors at the mall and assigned someone else to watch his house. Next time Jeffers goes in someplace like that, he's to be followed inside, and the officer on duty will call for backup to watch the car."

Gary dropped his gaze. "I'll notify everyone. Sorry,

Luke."

"We might have learned what other car he drove. He was probably there just before ten to retrieve it. Let's hope he was meeting his wife for dinner."

Luke hoped he wouldn't be notified of another death in a day or two.

~~~

Luke enjoyed his conversation with Shannon as they entered the wooded part of the track. He hadn't realized that she'd changed professions and become a massage therapist. He wondered if she had a craving for human contact after he'd abandoned her. That wasn't something he could ask her, but he hoped it wouldn't be long before he could give her all the physical contact and love she deserved.

"Why specialize in children?" He gave her a smile. When he'd left, she'd been working toward her teaching degree.

"Children don't always understand what's happening to them. I wanted to help them relax and get through whatever it is. I've taken some psychology classes, too. I'm by no means a psychologist, but I hope I at least help them deal with their situations as I massage them. I've got some autistic clients who are improving. They can handle touch much better than the first few times I saw them. The same with children who've been abused. The kids are mostly after school appointment. Massage is helpful to senior citizen, too."

"I'm glad you found something you really enjoy."

She frowned and turned her head away. "It helped me get through—everything."

Meaning him leaving, and the loss of their baby. Shannon had suffered so much. At least she'd found helping other people helped her.

Thinking about how Shannon had fallen apart at the loss of her baby, it must have been difficult to touch another child. "Was it hard at first—to massage the young ones?"

She blinked as if she was holding back tears, and he wished he could take his question back. "The first baby I massaged, I cried. I'm glad it was during our class so someone else could take over."

Luke glanced at her, and a patch of red behind her caught his eye. He studied it. A body. He stopped abruptly, frowning. His heart hammered. This was where Shannon's body would have been dumped if the killer had succeeded.

Shannon ran a couple of more steps, stopped and turned back. "Luke, what's wrong?"

He bracketed her face with his hands. "Shannon, I don't want you to see it."

Fear shown from her eyes. She grabbed his wrists with trembling hands. "See what?"

"A body. I have to check it out. Stay here."

His hands moved with her head as she nodded. He released her and scanned the area before approaching the body. They were nearly through the woods, so the killer would likely have come from the direction they were headed. One more sweep assured that they appeared to be alone. Staying far from the disturbed leaves, he knelt beside the auburn-haired woman and touched the cold skin. She wore running clothes and shoes, and lay on her back, one hand resting on her stomach, and the other on the ground. She'd probably been there all night. There was no need to find a pulse, the neck was cut like all the others. He went back to Shannon.

Her fear-filled eyes were fixed on the body. "It's another victim of The Slasher, isn't it?" She wrapped her arms around herself and closed her eyes.

He drew Shannon into his side, and pulled out his phone, placing a call to the coroner, then one to Gary. He told them to park on the road in case there were tracks.

Her arms snaked around his waist. After he pocketed his phone. Shannon still trembled, so he tightened his hold.

Her voice was muffled as she said, "Her hair's the same color as mine."

"He didn't choose her because her hair matches yours, Shannon. He chose her and you because it matches someone else."

"When is he going to stop?"

"When we catch him."

Sirens approached, and shut off on the other side of the trees. Two officers jogged from the direction Luke and Shannon had been heading. They scanned the body then waited for Luke's instructions.

"I want each of you to go both ways down the path, far enough so nobody can see the body. Turn back anybody coming this way." They nodded and split up.

Gary and the coroner arrived together. "Gary, can I use your car to take Shannon home?"

"Sure." He tossed his keys to Luke.

Luke guided her to the end of the wooded area to the car. He u-turned and pulled into Shannon's driveway. They exited the car, and he took her key, opening the front door and pulled her inside. Once again, he wrapped his arms around her, and held her head against his chest.

"I'm so sorry you had to see that."

"I'd pushed it out of my mind." A shiver passed through Shannon, and he tightened his hold. "That could have been me." She strained back far enough to stare into his face. Her fear tightened his stomach. "Do you think he's still trying to get me?"

"I don't know, but we have to be careful." He ran a few strands of her hair through his fingers and smiled. "You could dye your hair blonde for a while."

Shannon dropped her head back to his chest. "It's probably too late for that."

Luke stepped away. "I don't want to leave you, but I've got to get back over there. Are you all right alone, or shall I call my mom or Will to stay with you?"

She closed her eyes, took a deep breath then stiffened her back. "I can handle this. You go do what you need to."

"All right." He gave her a gentle kiss, wishing she didn't have to handle another thing alone. "Lock up."

~~~

After twisting the lock, Shannon leaned back against the door and slid to the floor. Her legs wouldn't hold her any longer. The killer had been on her street again. He'd left that woman near the spot where he'd almost taken her. It was far too easy to imagine herself in that woman's place.

Tears slid down her face as she remembered a time when she wouldn't have cared if someone killed her. She couldn't have taken her own life, but she would have welcomed death—an end to her daily pain of loss. She didn't know how many months she lived as a ghost, barely surviving. Life went on around her, but didn't touch her. Caring for Willa was what first pulled her out of the dead space. She couldn't resist Willa's smiles and laughter. Her niece reached into Shannon's heart and mended it.

Now, she didn't want to be a killer's target. Alive, there was always hope.

She knew Luke cared for her. Maybe he only realized how much after he left. She was beginning to think she had to give Luke another chance for herself. She'd been getting through her days better, but she only started to really feel alive again after Luke came back. For good or bad, she needed to see where it led.

~~~

Luke strode to the coroner who squatted in front of the body. Dave had arrived and searched the ground, as Liz took a close-up picture of the bruised, slashed neck.

"Anything new, Sam?"

Sam glanced over his shoulder and stood. "It looks like The Slasher. I've got this." He lifted his hand to show Luke the driver's license he held by the edges.

Luke leaned closer. "Jeannette Atwater."

"She's—she was a lawyer," Gary said.

Turning to his assistant, Luke raised an eyebrow. "You knew her?"

Gary shook his head. "I've never talked to her, but I've seen her in court."

"Find out where her office is, notify whoever needs to be, and find out why she was left in this park."

Gary waved a hand at the body. "That last is pretty obvious with the outfit and shoes."

Luke glared at him. "There are at least twenty places she could have had her run. Maybe the killer didn't abduct her here. Maybe he abducted her somewhere else and left her here to tell me he could get to Shannon again."

Gary raised his hands. "All right, all right. I'm on it." He stalked away.

This murder was way too personal.

Chapter 17

Luke leaned over his desk, reading through his list of dates and time ranges for each of the murders. Jeffers could have done every one of them. He wouldn't even have arrived late for work on the day he attacked Shannon. But he would have been late if he'd succeeded and taken her to the lake house. Too bad the club owner hadn't kept track of Jeffers' arrivals at the golf club.

Three of the kidnappings were on Fridays after Jeffers got out of work. The third was a morning. After comparing the list, he stood and stretched.

Gary strode in. He pointed at Luke. "Sit back down."

He complied. "What's up?"

"You were right to have me find out why Jeannette Atwater was in the park. She wasn't there."

Luke raised his eyebrows. "What?"

"Yeah, I was surprised, too. Her running partner—" He checked his notes. "—Melanie Fox, was sick day before yesterday, so Jeannette ran alone. But they always ran at Briar Park, not Oak Street Park."

"She ran alone in a different park? With a killer running loose, she should have skipped her run, not change parks."

"She didn't change parks. I found her car at Briar Park."

"The killer broke his pattern. For me. He wanted me to be the one to find her." He slammed his fist on the desk. "He knows Shannon and I run there. He's taunting me, showing me that he can still get to her." He sucked in his breath.

"What?" Gary leaned forward.

"He's telling me that Jeannette always ran with a partner, but he got her anyway. Shannon always runs with a partner, and he's promising to get her, too."

"Why is he making this personal?"

"Because I made it personal by protecting Shannon after his first attempt. If this is Jeffers, and at this point I don't doubt it, he knows I'm closing in, and he's angry that he's a suspect. Maybe he figures I'll mess up the case if I'm too worried about Shannon."

~~~

Saturday morning, Shannon was nervous about her run, considering what they'd found the last time. Every time she thought of the body at the park, she imagined her own face on it.

She paused at her front door. Luke would be on the other side, like every morning she ran. If he wasn't, she wouldn't run. She opened the door, relief flooding her at the sight of Luke stretching, and she stepped onto the porch. "Good morning. Um, is it okay for us to run?"

He gripped her arm more firmly than she expected, but not painfully. "It's fine since you're not running alone." His grip tightened for a moment. "Don't ever run alone until we catch this guy."

He seemed as worried as the day she'd been attacked. "There's more, isn't there?"

He glanced over her shoulder then back at her face and let out his breath. "Yeah." His gaze darted across the street and back to her again. He always seemed aware of their surroundings, but his gaze didn't rest anywhere for more than a couple of seconds. The hairs on the back of her neck rose.

"The killer put the body in the park for me to find." His hand tightened on her arm. "Be extra careful, Shannon." He released her arm then hugged her close. "I don't want anything to happen to you."

His voice held anguish. She stood stiffly for a few moments, then tentatively put her arms around him. It felt good to be held like this, like it used to be. He did care what happened to her, at least right now. But would it last? He'd already proved he could love her and still betray her.

She stepped back, out of his arms, and faced the street. She didn't see a way he could prove he'd changed. "Let's run."

Shannon chattered about everything she could think of as Luke ran beside her. Anything, to not think about what they'd found the last time they'd run. She slowed when they approached the end of the wooded area. When she realized what she was doing, she sped up to get past the dreaded place.

Despite her best efforts, her gaze was drawn to the police tape blocking the area. Beyond that, there was the body and the trampled grass. She stumbled, staring at the spot. No, there was no body, just tape blocking where it'd been. Would she ever be able to run through these woods without thinking about that dead woman?

"Shannon, let's go."

His muffled voice dragged her back to the present. His hand on her arm, and the concern on his face penetrated the block of fear gripping her. Her lips were cold, and she trembled. She was almost surprised that her legs still held her up.

"I just need to get out of the woods." She stared down the path, but her feet were glued to the gravel. Luke took her hand and tugged. She stretched one foot out and then the other. Finally, she was running and broke into the sunshine again. Her body warmed, but she wouldn't release his hand. It threw off her rhythm, but she needed his touch, his warmth, his caring.

As they approached Shannon's house, Luke had mixed feelings about the run. He was saddened that Shannon had been fearful as they passed where they'd found the body, but it emphasized the danger she was in. The highlight for him was that she accepted his offer of support by holding his hand. She hadn't let go until they were well out of the woods.

Shannon unlocked her door. "Do you want to come in? I've got some ice-cold lemonade."

Luke studied her before responding, not sure if she was afraid to be alone. Did she need him or any warm body? It didn't matter. He'd show her every way he could that this time, he would be here for her. "Yes. Thanks." He followed her into the house and, as she went to the kitchen, he did a few cool down exercises just inside the door.

Luke straightened up from stretching to the floor. Shannon stood in the kitchen doorway, ice clinking in the glasses in her hands. He recognized the desire in her eyes. The last time he'd seen it, they'd ended up in bed together. That wouldn't happen today, but it gave him hope. Right now, she needed his support without clouding their issues with sex. He wouldn't take advantage.

She swallowed, blinked and stared over his shoulder. "Do you want to sit on the deck with these?"

He didn't want her to regret asking him. One false move would have her scurrying away. He'd have to tread carefully.

"Sounds nice." As he stepped toward her, she spun and led the way to the sliding glass doors in the dining room.

Luke stepped around her. "Here, let me get that." He unlocked and slid the door open and closed it behind them. Half of the deck was shaded by a large maple tree, and Shannon set the glasses on the table under it. They sat across from each other. He chugged half the drink, then tipped his head back, willing himself to take it slow. A slight breeze blew hair across his forehead.

He checked out the yard. Three sides were bordered with a six-foot stockade fence. "Friendly neighbors, huh?"

She smiled. "They are, actually. The ones on the left have a big dog that barks when he sees anything, so the fence keeps him quiet."

"You shouldn't be out here alone until the killer is caught."

Her glass clinked when she set it down too hard, her chin quivering. "I can't be in my own yard?"

"It's private back here. Anything could happen, and nobody would see." He hated frightening her, but she needed to think about every situation she might be in. It could save her life.

She used to live in a tiny apartment, and now owned a two-bedroom house. Wedges of flowers filled the corners of the yard. An eight-foot circle of flowers dominated the middle with a birdbath and birdfeeder, at its center. A stone path led to them.

"Was the yard like this when you bought the house?"

"No. It was mostly overgrown bushes and weeds. I decided to start fresh. They were really helpful at the garden shop."

When he and Shannon dated, she exclaimed over flower gardens, but had never shown an interest in having her own. Would she have grown into the same interests had they stayed together? Or was working in nature her way of coping with her double loss?

They talked of her work, not his, and movies they'd seen. He steered her away from talking about Willa because that might lead to talk of Sherry.

When Shannon no longer twisted her hands or gave the chair arms a death grip, Luke thought he could safely leave her. He drained his glass.

"Do you want more?" Shannon's words burst out. He couldn't tell if she was afraid to be alone, or if she didn't want him to leave.

He shook his head. "I've got to get home. Mom's watching Sherry, and she has plans. Will you be all right? You could come with me." The invitation had tumbled out without a thought.

Her mouth hung open. He'd shocked her. He wished he could call the words back.

She set her glass on the table, and hunched back in her chair, wrapping her arms around herself. "I can't. I'll be fine here."

Her words were like an arrow to his heart. He'd felt like part of a couple for the first time in four years, but they weren't.

He stood. "I want you locked inside before I leave."

Chapter 18

Luke's desk phone rang. He noted the time as he picked it up. Almost six-thirty, he really should have left the office already, but he got lost in reviewing every bit of evidence they had on the serial killer case. It was a good thing his mom had picked up Sherry for him.

"Luke Cade."

"Luke?"

Luke's stomach clenched. "Will?" There could be no good reason for Will to call.

"Luke, I don't know where Shannon is, and I didn't know who else to call." Panic filled his voice.

Luke's stomach clenched tighter. "She's missing?" Luke stood so fast his chair flew back and hit a filing cabinet with a crash. "What happened?"

"She was supposed to come over for dinner tonight. When she was twenty minutes late, I called her cell then her work phone and didn't get answers."

With each word, Luke grew colder.

Will rushed his next words. "I drove to her house, but she wasn't there. I went to her work. The security guard said she left at five-twenty."

Luke's chest was so tight, he could hardly draw in a breath. He slammed his fist into his chest.

"Luke, her car's still in the lot. Her purse was on the seat and the door unlocked." He rasped in a breath. "Do you think…he took her?"

Luke covered his eyes and slid his hand down his face.

All those early morning runs to protect her had done nothing. Each day, as he broke bit-by-bit through her walls, he fell more in love with the strong woman she'd become. And now, he might not see her alive again.

He had to find Shannon before anything worse happened to her. She could be dead already, but he didn't think so. She was last seen an hour ago. Her chances were better than all the other women. He blinked away tears and took several deep breaths. He needed control over his emotions.

"Luke?"

"Sorry, Will." He tried to put confidence in his voice. "We've been closing in. I have an idea where she might be."

"Thank God. You've got to find her before..." His voice cracked. "Just find her, please."

"I'll do my best." He wanted to promise to find her alive, but no matter how much he needed it to be true, he couldn't make that promise.

One of the first murder cases he'd worked on, he was sure they'd arrested the killer. Then days after the arrest, the case unraveled. In order to make a stronger case, Luke's more experienced partner hadn't stopped investigating and uncovered a scheme to frame the person they'd arrested.

There was a possibility that Jeffers was being set up. A killer might have followed Jeffers' schedule to throw suspicion on him. They hadn't found hair matching the victims in his car, but they had a witness who'd seen him with red haired women at the family's vacation home. It wasn't likely he was simply cheating on his wife.

Luke dropped the phone in its cradle and raced from his office. Gary wasn't at his desk. He dialed Gary's number on his cell phone and continued for the door. There was no time to stop and explain to anyone else.

"Yeah, Luke?"

"Shannon's been taken."

"Are you sure? It's only been two weeks."

"He's probably been watching her since Jeannette Atwater and saw his chance. Get a search warrant for Jeffers' lake house. You've got enough info for probably cause. Then meet me there." He climbed into his car. "Call in some of the others. And no sirens!"

"I will, and I'll be there as soon as I can."

He didn't know if the killer came back for Shannon because Luke was lead on The Slasher investigation. Maybe if he'd arranged for someone else to run with her, she'd be safe now. Or the killer may have always planned to try for Shannon again.

Taking a couple of deep breaths, Luke rolled his shoulders. He needed a clear head to save her. He tamped down his fear and tried, but failed, to treat this as any other case. A stupid move could cost Shannon's life.

~~~

Shannon's head hurt worse than it ever had before. She'd never had a migraine, but if this was one, now she knew why people found them debilitating. The light creeping between her eyelids was fairly bright, so she didn't want to test it by opening her eyes. A sudden throb dragged a groan from her which increased the pain. She tried to rub her forehead, but her hand jerked to a stop. What? She tugged, then opened her eyes, and froze. Scratchy rope tied her wrists to a metal headboard.

Her heart beat faster than if she'd been running. The only sound in the room was her breath sawing in-and-out. This was all kinds of bad. She vaguely remembered leaving work, opening her car door and being zapped by electricity. The headache was from hitting her head when she fell or from that horrible chemical she'd been forced to breathe.

The killer had her!

She yanked on the ropes. It didn't matter that her wrists were rubbing raw. That was nothing compared to a slashed throat. She had to break free, or she'd be like all those other women who lost their lives to The Slasher.

A high, small window suggested she was in a basement, although the room was finished. It wasn't dark out yet, so she'd been unconscious less than three hours. Overhead, fluorescent lights, in a drop ceiling, illuminated the room, leaving no shadowed corners. There were even pictures on the walls, calming forest and river scenes, doing nothing to reduce her fear.

She'd never thought about where the women were murdered, but a cozy, country room wouldn't have been in her top five. She would have expected a dilapidated cabin in the woods.

She lay on a bed with plastic under her. It would prevent blood from getting on the mattress. Her blood. Shivers wracked her.

Her bare shoulders were cold from the damp air. A light blanket covered her body. She shuffled her feet and found they were unbound, but that wouldn't help her escape. Her wiggling exposed her breasts, and goose bumps rose on her skin. He'd stripped her. She squeezed her eyes closed and tossed her head back and forth at the thought that he'd touched her while she was unconscious. She didn't want to think about it, but very soon it would be worse. She'd be conscious while he…

Tears slid down her face. She was going to die a horrible death and there was nothing she could do to stop it. All those other women couldn't prevent a monster from taking their lives. Even a police officer hadn't been able to save herself.

Shannon clamped her lips together. If the killer was here now, maybe he was waiting for her to wake up before hurting her. Any small thing she could do to delay her torture and death was worth trying.

She didn't want to die. In the last few weeks, she'd been more alive than she'd been in years. And now, when her heart was ready to start over, her life would be snuffed out. Luke would fall apart when he got the call that they'd found her body.

If she somehow survived this, she'd take a chance with him. She loved him. She'd buried it so deep she'd thought it was gone, but each time she saw Luke, it blossomed more.

Their lives would have been better if he'd discussed Annie's problems with her, and they could have come up with a solution together. She still didn't agree with the action he took, but she'd decided she could forgive him. Now, she'd never get to tell him.

More silent tears slipped from her eyes. She wouldn't make it out of this. No one knew where she was. Will probably thought she was running behind. By the time he realized she was missing, it'd be too late.

She stared wide-eyed at the open door when footsteps ran down the stairs. Her heart beat in her throat, and she couldn't catch her breath. Her body shook. She'd never known this kind of dread before. The fear of the man she escaped from in the park was nothing compared to this terror.

She scrunched her eyes closed, but snapped them back open, needing to see the face of the man who would torture her and take her life.

The man stopped in the doorway and smiled. It wasn't an evil smile. If she'd seen him on the street, she would have thought he was friendly. "You're awake. Now the fun can begin."

She shook her head vigorously. "No! Please don't."

"Ah, Shannon."

She stiffened at her name on his lips, her eyes widening.

Had he known who she was from the beginning?

"I've waited a long time to have you. Anticipation is going to make this so much sweeter."

She struggled, yanking her arms, kicking her feet. When the blanket slipped lower, his eyes gleamed, and she froze.

He took slow, deliberate steps toward her. He lifted his hand, and she forgot to breathe when light bounced off the blade of an X-Acto knife. He twisted his hand as he watched her. His face didn't look friendly any longer. He'd torture her and then he'd use that knife to kill her. She wanted to close her eyes, block out everything, go into a black hole in her mind where she couldn't see, hear, or feel anything. She couldn't. If there was a chance, however slim, that she could stop him, she needed her eyes open to do it.

He set the knife on the nightstand, and unbuckled his belt, unsnapped his jeans, slid down the zipper.

Cold shivers consumed her. He caressed her breast. Her stomach churned.

"You look the most like her of all," he whispered.

"Who? Why are you doing this?" Her voice shook as her tears returned.

He pulled a condom from his pocket, then kicked off his shoes. He pushed his pants down and stepped out of them. When he put a knee on the bed, Shannon kicked, aiming for his testicles. He blocked it then straddled her. She jerked her thighs up, trying to knock him off balance, but with no effect. He tore open the package and covered himself.

It was really going to happen. Up to this point, she'd had a small glimmer of hope that Luke, the police, or someone would save her. Now all hope was gone, and full-blown panic set in. Shannon screamed, "No! No! Stop!" She bucked to try to knock him off.

He laughed and hit her at the back of her calves causing her feet to fly out, so she dropped back to the bed. He slid down between her legs. "I love the feisty ones."

~~~

Luke drove past the lake house. A light was on inside the front of the house. Jeffers' car sat beside the back porch. He imagined Jeffers carrying Shannon inside as Paige Wallace had described the other women. No! He prayed he wasn't too late. He couldn't lose her now. He wouldn't lose her.

He parked a hundred feet down the road, got out and closed the door with barely a click. He'd done hostage recovers before, but worry for the victims was nothing like the panic he had to tamp down this time.

He ran back toward the house in the grass beside the road. At the property line, he crept along the edge of the woods in case he had to duck and hide. Every second counted, but he couldn't alert Jeffers to his presence. He worked at controlling his breathing, knowing it would keep the anxiety down.

Staying low, he ran to the Lexus and surveyed the interior. Plastic lined the back seat and floor. No wonder he hadn't gotten any evidence from Jeffers' car. A more thorough police search would find something.

At the front of the car, a basement light caught his attention. He didn't want to waste time looking through it, but if he saw Shannon, he'd know where to find her and have every right to go inside. If he didn't see her, he'd still go in.

He squatted next to the window, and leaned in, his nose nearly touching the glass. His breath froze. Shannon. Her eyes were closed, but there was no blood. A blanket covered the lower have of her body, leaving her bare breasts exposed. She swallowed. Alive. He let out his breath. There was still time.

He backed away, and sprinted to the back porch, and

crept across it to the door. It was locked. With his lock pick, the lock twisted in just over a minute, and he slipped the pick back into his pocket. He hoped it wasn't a crucial delay.

The urge to race inside to rescue Shannon almost overwhelmed him, but if he didn't do this right, it could get her killed. He dragged in two slow breaths, readied his gun, opened the door, and stepped inside.

Light from the living room dimly lit the kitchen, leaving shadows that someone could hide in. He debated his next move. A search of the main floor would be normal procedure, but if his quarry was in the basement with Shannon, he might hear Luke's footsteps above him. Only steps away, a closed door beckoned. It might be a pantry or lead to the basement. The cold knob turned without a sound, and he cracked the door open an inch.

Shannon screamed. "No! No! Stop!"

Luke's heart pounded painfully. He couldn't race down the stairs or Jeffers might hear him and kill Shannon before he reached her. Drawing in a deep breath, he descended the stairs, fast but quiet. He reached the bottom, relieved no steps had squeaked. The bed creaked and Jeffers laughed. Luke took long, careful strides toward the sound. A hand slapped flesh and he cringed.

"I love the feisty ones." Definitely Jeffers' voice.

After what felt like an agonizing hour, Luke reached the partially open door, and peeked in. Jeffers lay propped on his elbows between Shannon's legs.

Rage welled up inside Luke. He wouldn't let this killer hurt Shannon further. He threw the door open and launched himself at Jeffers. They rolled on the floor on the far side of the bed. Jeffers got in a weak punch to Luke's shoulder, but Luke was in no mood for a long brawl with him. He rammed the side of his gun into jaw Jeffers' jaw, followed with a left to the ribs, and then slammed the gun into the side of Jeffers head. The man went limp.

Luke got up, shoved Jeffers to his stomach and cuffed his hands behind his back. He drew in a couple breaths and willed his heart to slow. Shannon was alive. She was safe. He turned to Shannon.

She'd curled into a tight ball. He sat on the edge of the bed and she flinched. "Shannon, you're safe now." He picked up the blanket from the floor and tucked it around her, then with shaking fingers, he worked on the knots at her wrists.

It tore him up to see her tear-stained face, and the fear still in her eyes.

"Luke, you found me. I can't believe you found me. I didn't think I'd ever see you again." As soon as he released her, she wrapped her arms around him, her cold body trembling.

"Did he..." The most important thing was that she was alive.

"No. But almost..." She shivered, and buried her head in his neck. He tightened his arms around her.

"I'll find your clothes."

"No, don't leave me." Her arms held tighter.

He scanned the room. "Look, Shannon. Your clothes are on that table. Let's get you dressed before the police arrive." She glanced at Jeffers before nodding and dropping her arms.

He hurried to the table and returned, handing her the clothes. "Can you put them on yourself? I'll turn my back."

She nodded. "Can you hold up the blanket in case...?" Her gaze rested momentarily on Jeffers and back to him. He helped her from the bed and they adjusted the blanket. Clothing rustled, and her breath rasped. "Okay, I'm done."

He dropped the blanket and she wrapped her arms around him again.

"I have to keep an eye on him until the others arrive, but let's step into the other room." She nodded, and he led her through the doorway.

The tension left her body. The adrenalin rush was ending, and soon, she'd be exhausted.

Will! He was probably more frantic than when he'd called Luke.

He pulled out his phone, and Shannon frowned at him. "I have to call Will."

She raised an eyebrow.

Yeah, a lot had changed in the last couple of hours. "He called me in a panic because you didn't arrive for dinner." He flipped through his address book, realizing he didn't have Will's number.

"Can I talk to him?" He handed the phone to her.

She punched in the numbers and held the phone to her ear. "Will?" Will's voice was loud enough to hear the panic, but not his words. "Luke found me. I'm safe, but I can't talk right now." She handed the phone to Luke and wrapped her arms around him. "He wants to talk to you."

He held her tighter, protectively. "Hi, Will."

"Luke, thank God you found her. He didn't—"

Luke shivered at the close call. "No, she's all right. I got to her in time."

Will let out a heavy sigh. "I've never been so scared in my life."

"You and me both. I've got to finish up here. I'll bring Shannon to your place as soon as I can."

He called up his partner's number. "Gary, she's safe. Jeffers is cuffed. Are you almost here?"

"Best news I've heard in months. I'm just pulling up out front. The team shouldn't be far behind."

"Come to the basement. The back is open."

He handed his phone back to Shannon. "Now leave a message at your office to cancel your appointments for the next two days."

She started to protest, but he covered her lips. "You need some time to get over this." He waved his hand. "Believe me." She nodded and left the message.

A few minutes later, Shannon tensed and her gaze shot to the ceiling as if she might see who made the footsteps overhead.

"It's just Gary," Luke reassured her.

Feet clattered down the basement steps and Gary stopped at the bottom. He grinned and strode up to them. "Shannon. It's good to see you." He kept a bit of distance between them.

"Hi, Gary." She snuggled her head into Luke's neck.

Gary glanced at Luke. "Is he alive?"

Luke nodded.

"That's too bad. Where is he?" Gary scanned the room, and his gaze stopped on the doorway of the lit room.

Luke tipped his head towards it. "In there. I knocked him out."

As Gary passed them, he dropped a hand on Luke's shoulder. "Good job, Luke." A grunt came from the other room and Gary said, "Oh, man, he *was* close."

Shannon shivered, and Luke held her tighter, kissing the top of her head. He didn't ever want Shannon to go through again the kind of terror she'd experience over the last few hours.

More feet clattered overhead, then down the stairs.

Luke nodded. "Hey, Dave, you're sure to find evidence here. Sam, fortunately you're not needed this time, but would you mind waiting a few minutes?"

He stopped beside them. Luke touched Shannon's arm. "Will you be all right if I go in there and talk to Gary for a couple of minutes? Sam can wait with you here."

Worry filled her eyes but she nodded and released him. He hated to leave her, but needed to give Gary some information.

Luke stepped into the other room. Jeffers was conscious and they'd managed to get his pants on him.

"Gary?"

He glanced up, and Luke motioned him into the corner.

"I'm leaving with Shannon. We'll come in the morning to interview. I just wanted you to put into your report what I found when I arrived." Gary nodded and scribbled while Luke described what he saw and what he did.

"Oh, and Jeffers abducted her from the parking lot where she works." He answered a few questions.

Luke glanced at Shannon and back to Gary. "Sorry to ask this of you, but after he's booked, can you call his wife?" He nodded toward Jeffers.

"Sure. It's going to be tough on her."

Yeah. There was no easy way to tell a woman her husband had killed seven women, all because they had red hair like her.

Chapter 19

In the doorway of Will's home, Shannon hugged Leah and clung to Will. For a short time, she thought she'd never see them again. More accurately, they'd never see her again. She'd been as close to death as when she'd lost the baby. For the second time, Will was her savior. He'd gotten her to the hospital in time when she miscarried, and he'd called Luke when he couldn't find her. She hugged him tighter for a second before releasing him, then wiped the tears from her cheeks.

The kids had been tucked into bed already, or she'd be hugging them just as hard. They probably hadn't been told that she'd been missing, preserving their innocence. She squeezed her eyes closed. She couldn't imagine the pain of telling a child that someone they love had died.

Will held his hand out to Luke. "Thank you for finding her." His voice cracked.

Luke shook Will's hand, then wrapped his other arm around Will's shoulder. A second's hesitation, and Will's arm came around Luke and thumped him on the back. Nothing like bringing his sister back alive to start mending fences.

Luke stepped back and gave Shannon's hand a squeeze. "I was almost too late."

He swiped his eyes, and Shannon wrapped her arm around his waist, resting her head on his chest. "But you weren't." He'd been tough and determined while he took down the killer and talked to the other officers. She wasn't surprised that he finally gave in to his emotions afterward.

He pulled her closer.

Will touched her shoulder. "We have the guest room made up for you."

Shannon shivered at the thought of trying to fall asleep all alone and waking up in a strange bed, and shook her head. "No. I want to go home." She tipped her head back, stared into Luke's eyes. "If you'll come stay with me."

She needed to be tucked into her own bed, and wake up there in the morning, but she couldn't stay alone tonight. She needed her protector. She didn't know how she could be both keyed up and about to fall asleep standing. She was sure that once she got to her own bed, she'd relive being in that death bed for half the night.

"Of course. Let me have Mom keep Sherry." He called his mother. "Mom, can you take Sherry home with you? Shannon needs me with her tonight." He paused. "I'll explain more tomorrow."

Will glared at Luke. "I don't think that's a good idea. She should be with her family after what's happened to her."

Shannon squeezed her brother's arm. "Will, it's all right. We've been working things out."

He frowned at her and lowered his voice. "Shannon, are you sure?"

She squeezed his hand. "We'll talk more about it later, but yes, I'm sure."

She hugged Will and Leah. "I'll call tomorrow."

Luke led her to his car. Glancing around, she realized it was dark, and she had no idea how late. A lifetime had passed in a matter of hours. She'd nearly died. If the killer had succeeded in kidnapping her the first time he'd tried, it wouldn't have ended with her rescue. Luke hadn't gathered enough information to know where to look for her. She would have been raped, tortured, and killed like the other women.

Fear pounded through her. When that man entered the room, she'd lost hope. She'd fought him, knowing it would only postpone her death. The others hadn't been as fortunate as her. They'd suffered what she could only imagine. She froze, and curled a hand over her mouth trying to hold in the sobs.

Luke wrapped his arms around her and backed her against the car. She pressed her face into his chest.

"It's all right. I've got you. Let it out."

Over and over, his words flowed through her. She stopped hearing them, but the reassuring rumble in his chest, made her feel safe. She cried for the women who'd suffered and died for nothing more than having the wrong hair color. They didn't deserve to have their lives cut short.

She became conscious of Luke's hand running over her head and neck repeatedly. His hoarse words grounded her, brought her back to the present, to life.

Shannon sniffled, drew in a deep, cleansing breath, and tipped her head back. Luke stared down at her. Her fear was his fear. The streetlight at the corner caught a gleam on his cheeks. She ran her fingers over one damp cheek and rubbed her thumb across them. He'd cried for her, for them.

He kissed her fingers, and spoke barely above a whisper. "Ready to go now?"

She nodded, her throat too tight to speak. Exhaustion turned everything into slow motion. He buckled her in, then climbed into the driver's seat. She leaned into him and rested her head on his arm.

In a few minutes, he turned into her driveway. For a moment, she wondered where her car was, and fear gripped her when she remembered why it was still at work.

Luke wrapped an arm around her shoulders. "Shannon, you're safe now."

As soon as they entered her house, she hugged him. She

hadn't been able to let him go for more than a few minutes at a time. She took in his weary, loving eyes.

"Luke, I need you to hold me while I sleep. I'm afraid I'll have nightmares."

His lips barely touched hers, and she clung to him.

"You and me, both. I won't be able to sleep unless you're in my arms, so I know you're safe. If you have any bad dreams, I'll help you through them." He gave her a lop-sided smile. "Will you do the same for me?"

She hugged him tighter and nodded. "I need a shower. I smell like..." A shiver passed through her. She needed to feel clean again, and hoped a shower would be enough.

They entered her bedroom, and she drew comfort from the familiar space. The quilt her grandmother had made her that she'd packed away until she found her own apartment. The solid maple bedroom set that she'd bought at a used fur-niture store. The treasured mementos on the dresser.

Luke sat on the bed and leaned back on his arms. "I'll wait here."

She nodded and stepped into the bathroom. She was alone, like when she'd woke up in that basement. She lifted her hands. Her wrists were raw, but no rope confined her. At a touch, the door on the tub glided open. Once in the shower, it would be a barrier between them, somehow increasing her distance from Luke. But he was only ten steps away. Not far, but out of sight. He might have gone to the kitchen and wouldn't be able to hear her. She had to check, and stepped back into the bedroom.

He sat on the bed where she'd left him. Moments ago. Only moments?

Her voice croaked. "Can you come with me? I can't stay in there alone."

He was by her side in a second and touched her face. "I'll stay in the bathroom with you, but not in the shower."

He kissed her forehead.

He sat on the counter, and leaned against the mirror as she stripped and adjusted the water. She stole glances at him, and each time his eyes were closed. After she was under the spray, Luke talked to her. The words didn't register, but the sound of his voice soothed her. Warm water slid down her body, relaxing her, letting the exhaustion leak into her bones. Soaping up her sponge, she scrubbed every inch of her body, rinsed and did it again. She turned off the water and grabbed a towel from the bar on the shower door. She dried and wrapped the towel around herself.

Luke hopped off the counter and touched her shoulder. "Do you want to wait here while I shower?"

She nodded. He lifted her onto the counter and gave her a soft kiss before dropping his clothes. He stepped into the shower and adjusted the water. She liked watching him run his hands over his body, but more than that, he was here for her.

Luke dried, and put his boxers back on. He slid her off the counter, picked up their clothes, and headed to the bedroom.

Shannon followed him, opened a drawer, and took out a nightgown. She dropped it over her head, and tugged the towel off from underneath. The gown was sleeveless, thin cotton that came nearly to her knees. She stifled a yawn.

Being home was helping. Having Luke with her helped even more.

"You need sleep." He threw back the covers and slid into bed. He scooted to the middle and held out his hand.

She was suddenly nervous and caught her lip between her teeth. They hadn't shared a bed in years.

"Come on. We'll spoon."

She sat on the bed and scooted back until she bumped into him, then lay down on her side. Luke reached around her waist and snuggled her closer and she relaxed against him.

"Thank you," she whispered. His warmth at her back relaxed her more than the shower had, and she drifted off to sleep.

~~~

Luke opened his eyes to daylight, Shannon still pressed warmly against him. Sometime during the night, she'd whimpered and thrashed, and he'd comforted her. Whispered soothing words, rubbed her arms, until she drifted back to sleep.

She stretched then snuggled into him.

Luke kissed the back of her neck. "Mmm. It's nice to wake up with you in my arms." Four long years of waking up alone, without the woman he loved. Just because she needed him the night before, didn't mean they'd overcome all that stood between them.

She squirmed around until she faced him.

"Don't do that unless you plan on following through," he told her.

She leaned forward, and grazed her lips across his. He kept his arm loosely around her, waiting for her to take the next step. He'd been there to give her comfort, but he wouldn't take advantage. It was a battle he'd lose if she didn't decide soon to make love or get out of bed.

She placed her hand on his cheek, and he kissed her palm, touching his tongue to it. She gasped. Maybe just a little nudge his way.

"Luke, first, I want to tell you I forgive you."

He sucked in a breath and closed his eyes. He didn't think he'd ever hear those words. Some part of his heart opened up, as if a small, clenched fist had relaxed. He gathered her closer. "Shannon."

138

"And second, I want us to make love because I love you and—"

He didn't need any more encouragement. His lips took hers, and he rolled onto his back, taking her with him. For their first time, he didn't want her having any flashbacks of the killer forcing himself on her.

She straddled his hips and shimmied out of her night-gown. He skimmed his hands along her hips and closed in on her breasts. They were fuller than when he'd last seen them, and her hips wider. He loved every inch of her.

For years, he'd buried all his memories of making love to Shannon. It'd been hard enough to live without her, he couldn't have done it if he'd allowed himself fantasies. Since he'd been back though, she'd starred in too many of his dreams.

He sat up and trailed kisses to her ear and tickled her earlobe with his tongue, enjoying the shiver that took her. "Lift up."

She raised up, and he laid back, slipping off his boxers. Leaning over the side of the bed, he picked up his pants and fished out a condom.

"Prepared, are you?"

He grinned as he rolled it on. "Since the day I responded to your 911 call." At that point, chances were slim that he'd ever need them with Shannon. All he had was hope, and a hunger to right his wrong.

She touched his face. "I'm glad you didn't give up on me. I understand how you felt responsible for Annie." She stuck her bottom lip out. "Even though I don't agree with your solution. And you didn't know I was pregnant because I didn't tell you. I can't blame that on you." She gave him a watery smile. "I should have screamed it at you, but I was shocked and hurt, and gave up."

He still blamed himself for not letting her speak when

she wanted to tell him she was pregnant. He never would have abandoned her, and they would have figured out Annie's situation together.

He hugged her tight. They'd lost four years because of his stupid knee-jerk fix for Annie, ignoring the most important person in his life. He didn't deserve Shannon, but he would show her everyday how important she was, and that he loved her. From now on, she would always be his first choice. "I'm sorry. I shouldn't have made that decision without you. You'll be a part of every big decision from now on."

Pulling her down to him, he kissed her. He ran his hands across her back and over her rounded butt. Slipping one hand between her legs, he found where she was most sensitive. Her legs clamped tighter against him, and he grinned. "Still like that, huh?"

"Luke, I need more."

He did, too. If only he'd realized that four years ago. "I love you." He grasped her hips and lifted her. She wrapped her hand around him, and pure magic shot through him. He groaned and rasped out, "Inside you, now." He wasn't about to come their first time without her.

She positioned him at her entrance and lowered a bit. They stared into each other's eyes as she eased down inch-by-inch. She was his Shannon, but more confident in herself. Once she was fully seated, he took her hands from her thighs and placed them on his shoulders.

"Giddy-up, cowgirl," he said with a grin.

Shannon lifted and dropped, making them both moan. She didn't take her gaze off him, and it turned him on more. Before, she would close her eyes, but he'd loved watching her come.

The pleasure zipped up his spine, but he wasn't doing this alone. He rubbed his fingers on her clit, and she clenched. Her breath huffed out as she sped up, her breasts swaying in front of him. Her eyes closed as pulses squeezed him. He gripped her hips and powered into her, coming seconds behind her.

Shannon flopped down on him, her arms circling his head. Between breaths, she kissed him. "We are definitely doing it like that again."

He chuckled. "Definitely. I'm not sure why we didn't before."

She raised her brows. "Maybe because you were always so eager to…taste me?"

"That must be it." He stuck the finger he'd used to excite her in his mouth and sucked. "Just how I remember." He ran the fingers from his other hand along her jaw and into her hair. No one was as special as her. If this was a dream, he hoped he'd never wake up. "Shannon, thank you for taking me back. I wasn't really living until I found you again."

"Me either, and I didn't even realize it."

He sat up, taking her with him. "As much as I want to spend hours with you here, we have to get to the police station."

She sighed then wiggled off his lap. "My shower's big enough for two."

Chapter 20

Shannon held tightly to Luke's hand as they entered the police station. The police needed her account of what happened, but she didn't want to relive the terror.

Everybody's gazes followed them as they passed through the desks to the interrogation room. Gary got up and followed. He closed the door, sat across from them and turned on a recorder.

Luke still held her hand. "Shannon, I'm going to walk you through what happened." He glanced at Gary. "Make sure I don't miss anything."

His eyes locked on her, and he rubbed his fingers over her hand. "What happened when you left work?"

She bit her lip. Maybe she could pretend it was a movie with a happy ending. But knowing the ending didn't make it easier. She stared at a gouge on the table. "I-I left the building about five-fifteen. I didn't see anyone. I passed a dark gray car and then an empty space, and got to my car. I opened the door, and tossed in my purse."

She shivered. She should have been more aware. "A car door opened behind me." She rubbed her arms, and Luke took her hand back. "It felt like an electrical charge went through me, and I fell. I heard my head hit something, but I didn't even feel it." It happened so fast, there'd been no time to be afraid.

"You lost consciousness?"

"Yes, but not from that. He slapped a cloth with some horrible chemicals over my mouth and nose. When I woke up, I was tied to the bed. Naked." For a moment, she was back on that bed with the crackling plastic. He'd stripped her. She didn't want to think what he might have done to her unconscious body. She trembled. Luke scooted closer and wrapped an arm around her shoulders.

"Was he there when you woke up?"

Her eyes remained fixed on the gouge in the table. "No. I was alone for maybe ten minutes." She blinked back tears. It was over. She wasn't going to die. He hadn't raped her, but she could feel his naked body on hers. "Luke!" Panic rose in her.

He twisted in his seat, dragged her onto his lap, and held her against his chest. "Shh. It's all right. You're safe now, Shannon."

She nodded her head against his shoulder. She could smell Luke, feel his warmth and strength. She took in a shuddering breath. The next one was easier. She pushed away. "I'm sorry. I'm okay now."

Luke took her hand again and squeezed it. "What happened when he came in?"

"He smiled when he saw I was awake."

"Did you recognize him?"

She shook her head. "H-he looked like a normal person. I kind of expected him to look like the monster he is. I don't remember seeing him before, but he said my name. He knew who I was."

She caught the grim expression Luke gave Gary.

"What happened next?" Luke almost whispered.

"He started walking toward me, and I panicked. I tried to break free and the blanket slipped off." She shivered.

"And then?"

She bit her lip. "He set down a knife and started to undress." She buried her face in Luke's neck for a second and inhaled his scent, letting it calm her.

143

Her gaze returned to the marred table. "He touched my breast and said I looked the most like her of all of them." Remembering the man's hand on her made her cringe.

Luke shared another silent exchange with Gary.

"I asked him who. I thought if I could get him to talk, it might delay…what he was going to do. But he didn't answer me." She dropped her eyes to their joined hands, wondering if she squeezed too hard. He didn't complain.

"I tried kicking him but he climbed on top of me." Thinking about it made her feel dirty. A full body convulsion shook her.

Luke tightened his arm around her. "I've got you. You're safe now."

She leaned into him, not able to hold back the tears. She stared into his eyes. "You saved me." She attempted a smile.

Luke plucked a tissue from a box on the table and wiped her cheeks. He glanced at Gary. "Have we missed anything?"

Gary turned off the recorder. "This should be good. I'm sorry, Shannon. You may have to testify in court."

She bit her lip, but nodded. It was hard telling it once. How many times would she have to repeat it before the trial? Then she'd have to tell a crowded courtroom how that man had touched her, what he'd almost done. She didn't want to do it. It would be better to forget, but she'd get through it to make sure the killer paid for the lives he'd taken, and never have the chance to do it again.

Luke tightened his arm around her. "Will you be all right in here if I leave you for a few minutes? I'll be right outside the door."

"I think so." He scooted her to the other chair.

~~~

Luke kept his voice down so other officers couldn't hear.

"How did Jeffers' interrogation go?"

"He wouldn't confess to anything."

"We need to check his previous addresses. See if there are any unsolved murders."

"I'll start that today. Oh, Mrs. Jeffers came in. She said she's not hiring a lawyer for him. I gave her a list of the dates the victims died and asked her to write down Jeffers' whereabouts for any of the dates that she could remember."

Gary walked away and Luke put his hand on the door-knob to go back to Shannon.

An officer touched his arm. "Luke."

"What's up?"

Leaning close, Richard kept his voice low. "There's a situation in the holding area."

Luke frowned at him. "Let me take Shannon to my office, and I'll be right there. Hey, Gary."

Gary stopped.

"Can you sit with Shannon in my office, talk to her? I have to go to the holding area."

Gary sauntered over, "Sure, no problem."

Luke opened the door. "Shannon, I have to check on something. I want you to wait for me in my office. I asked Gary to join you."

"But, Luke..." She made fists. "Okay. I can do this." Luke held out his hand, she stood and grasped it.

Once Shannon was settled into Luke's chair, he hurried to the holding area.

Two paramedics were talking to Richard. *That can't be good*. He approached them. "What's going on?"

"The coroner's in the cell." He nodded to the closest one.

"Jeffers?"

"Yeah."

Luke entered the cell as Sam bent over Jeffers body.

"Sam, what happened?"

His body. The man that had threatened and nearly killed Shannon couldn't hurt her anymore. She wouldn't have nightmares about him escaping prison and coming back to kill her. He was dead.

Sam stood. "Apparently, he hanged himself. I'll do an autopsy to make sure it was suicide." A torn sheet lay beside the body. "Richard found him and administered CPR, but it was too late."

Jeffers took his own life. Too bad he hadn't done it before he'd killed seven women.

Sam left the cell and Luke followed. "You can take him now," Sam told the paramedics. They nodded and rolled their stretcher into the cell.

Luke crossed his arms. "Tell me what happened, Richard."

"His wife visited. She told him she was divorcing him and never wanted to see him again. He tried to convince her he was innocent. She wasn't buying it."

Pointing to the cell, Luke asked, "So, when did this happen?"

"I took him back to his cell and checked on him twenty minutes later. He must have done it as soon as he got in there."

Luke sighed and slipped his hands into his pockets. "It's not what I expected from him. Well, it saves us building a case and having a trial."

Shannon. He needed to get back to her.

Voices murmured as he approached the door. Shannon saw him and stopped talking. Her eyes held his and she smiled, standing.

Gary stood. "Well, I guess I'll get back to my work."

"Stay for a minute," Luke said as he rounded his desk. He put his arm around Shannon, like coming home. She settled into him.

Gary raised his brows.

"It's about Jeffers. It's over."

"Over?"

"He killed himself after his wife visited."

Shannon jerked and gasped.

He stared into her precious eyes. "It's over. You won't need to testify. I'll help you put this behind us."

Some of the tension left her.

He spoke to the other man. "Gary, since you've already talked to Susan Jeffers, I want you to go back and tell her about her husband."

Gary rubbed the back of his neck and grimaced. "That's going to be rough. I'm not sorry he's dead. I know she said she planned to divorce him, but as of yesterday morning, she probably thought she was happily married."

"Yeah, sorry. I still want you to check his previous addresses. Notify authorities at those locations and ask if they want a DNA sample sent."

"Got it."

"Oh, and I won't be in until Monday." Gary probably figured out the reason for that immediately.

After Gary left, Luke turned Shannon to face him. "I've got about three hours until I have to pick up Sherry." He lowered his voice. "I'd love to make love with you."

Blushing, she lowered her eyes, but he noticed her breath quicken. She held her hand out.

Chapter 21

The door closed behind them and Shannon's nerves jangled. They'd made love that morning, but they were already in bed together, their bodies touching. And she'd told him for the first time since he got back that she loved him. They couldn't *not* make love.

This was...premeditated. They'd walk into her room, drop their clothes...they'd do it. Maybe she wasn't ready for this.

Luke stood behind her, so she turned to face him. "Luke."

He touched the side of her neck, slipped his hand to the back of her head, and pulled her to him. His lips claimed hers, and she wrapped her arms around his waist, their bodies feeding off each other's heat. This was where she needed to be, was supposed to be.

He pushed a little away. Confused, she opened her eyes and found concern in his. He grasped the hem of her shirt and slowly lifted it, probably giving her time to change her mind. She wouldn't. Not after that kiss calmed and excited her. She wanted this as much as he did.

He'd spent months running with her, keeping her safe. Showing her she was worth his time. He'd worked frantically to rescue her. And he'd cried with her.

Lifting her arms, she focused on his eyes. Determination, lust, but most of all love, touched her. As soon as her shirt cleared her head, she leaned into him and tipped her face up. She needed another of his warm kisses. She was supposed to be with him. She ran her hands up his sleek body and twined her hands around his neck.

He picked her up, carried her to the bedroom and set her down beside the bed. He feathered kisses over her as he removed her clothes.

He stepped back, locking eyes with her as he removed his shirt. Her fingers itched to run over his chest, his back, into his hair.

She riveted her gaze on his hands as he unbuckled his belt, opened the button, and so slowly lowered the zipper. She licked her lips. She glanced up to see his satisfied smile.

His tongue flicked across his lips. Maybe he was making fun of her. "Shannon, I love you."

He shoved his pants off his hips, and they slid to his knees. She'd followed every delicious inch. He lifted out one leg, then the other. She wished she was that sexy getting out of pants. She let her gaze wander up his muscular legs, hoping she teased him a little by taking so long to get to the main attraction.

He stood, with his hands at his hips, a finger under each side of his briefs. Her breath caught at how ready he was for her. He pushed the fabric down, freeing himself. She couldn't keep away any longer, and took that single step that brought them together.

She slid her hands to the back of his neck and kissed him. His firm chest met her soft breasts, her smooth thighs met his tough ones, and her stomach met his desire.

He scooped her up. "There was a time I didn't think I'd ever have you back. You've made me the happiest man in the world." He folded back the bedcovers and lowered her to the sheet, sliding in beside her.

His kisses and roving hands made her forget everything, except how much she wanted to make up for lost time, and show Luke the love that she'd buried, and he'd nurtured to grow again.

~~~

Shannon paced in Luke's living room. He'd left her there while he picked up Sherry. He wanted to tell her about Shannon before they met. She strode to the window and checked the driveway and street. Nothing yet. She retraced her steps from one end of the room to the other, more nervous than before they'd made love.

She wondered if the furniture had been picked out by Annie. None of it was the furniture he'd had in his apartment before he'd left. She peeked into the other rooms until she found his bedroom. The bed and nightstands were the ones she remembered. The dresser that always had stuck drawers had been replaced with one the same color as the bed and stands.

This hyper anxiety was worse than waiting for a job interview. Probably worse than a young man about to talk to his girlfriend's father about marriage. She stopped. Was that it? Did she feel like she was interviewing for the job of substitute mother? Did she need to get approval from Sherry to marry her father?

They hadn't talked about marriage. They'd talked about a lot of things, but not a relationship. Years ago, that's where she thought they were headed, but that wasn't how it turned out. She resumed her pacing. Now that she'd figured out why she was nervous, she became even more nervous. What if Sherry didn't like her? That would affect her relationship with Luke. Some couples broke up when stepchildren made trouble.

If that happened, Luke would have to choose his daughter. She hoped it didn't. Once before, he'd chosen Annie and Sherry. She didn't want there to be a choice. This time, she wanted it to work out that he could have both Sherry and her.

She dealt with children daily during massage therapy. Some were resistant at first, and she coaxed them into letting her touch them, sometimes over a few sessions, starting with extremities and working toward the body.

She could treat this in a similar fashion. Take it slow. Work step by step through any resistance.

A car stopped in the driveway. She paused halfway across the living room floor and stared at the door. Minutes passed or was it hours? The door opened, and her already tense muscles tightened even more.

She relaxed just a little when Luke smiled at her. He was holding Sherry, one of her arms wrapped around his neck. Sherry peeked at her then buried her blonde head into her father. He whispered to her as he continued to walk toward Shannon. The little head nodded.

It was no surprise he was a loving father. And his daughter loved him just as much. For a second, pain twisted her heart as she thought about the love Luke would have given their child. She blinked back the sudden sting of tears and smiled at him.

He stopped in front of her, took her hand with his free one and squeezed. "Shannon, I'd like you to meet Sherry." Sherry peeked at her from the corner of her blue eye. "Sherry, this is Shannon."

Shannon held out her hand. Sherry glanced at her father, and he nodded. She slowly reached out her hand. The small, warm one was gobbled up by her larger, cool one.

The only part of the cute munchkin that resembled her father was her chin.

"It's nice to meet you, Sherry." Shannon's nerves calmed. Sherry was a small child who had been through a lot of heartache in her short life.

Luke lifted Sherry higher. "Remember how I told you

Shannon is special?" Sherry more fully faced Shannon and nodded. "There's something else special about her. Her brother is Willa's father."

Sherry gasped and smiled. "You know Willa? She's my best friend."

Shannon nodded. "She's my niece."

"Are you Aunt Shannon?"

Shannon nodded.

"Willa told me you did fun stuff with her."

"You can join us the next time we do something fun together." She smiled. Knowing the right people made all the difference.

Sherry clasped her hands. "I can?"

Shannon nodded.

"Are you going to be my new mom?"

How could she answer that? Her eyes darted to Luke.

He smiled at Shannon, lifted her hand to his mouth and kissed it. "Yes, she is."

"Was I just proposed to by a five-year-old?"

Luke's smile widened. "Yes. And her father. Marry me, Shannon."

She blinked back tears. Luke dropped her hand, wrapped his arm around her waist and pulled her next to his daughter. He kissed her lips. Not a sexy kiss this time, but his love was in it.

Beside her ear a small voice said, "Daddy never did *that* to Mommy."

Shannon smiled against his lips and Luke pulled back. He whispered, "You didn't answer."

She laughed. "You didn't give me a chance. Yes, I'll marry you." She gave him another kiss.

"Next week."

"What?" Seriously? She'd only been officially talking to him for a short time.

He rushed on. "We'll have a ceremony in your backyard. I'll find a justice of the peace. We'll have just family and a few friends." Were his eyes really begging? "I've wasted so much time, Shannon. I don't want to waste any more."

"All right. Next Saturday."

"Can I wear a pretty new dress?" a perky voice asked.

Shannon had almost forgotten that Sherry was there.

Luke laughed. "Yes, sprite, you can." He set Sherry on the floor. "Why don't you go play for a little bit while Shannon and I work out the details, then we'll go out to dinner?"

"McDonald's?"

"Um, probably not."

Sherry marched then threw her hands in the air. "He always says no!"

Shannon smothered a laugh.

"I'll call Mom. Maybe she can help Sherry find a dress."

Shannon nibbled her lip. "Would you mind if I took Sherry to find a dress? Maybe I can take Willa, too."

Luke smiled and kissed her. "That would be great. Kind of bonding time, huh?"

"Yeah, a little bonding before we marry would be good. Will your mom be surprised?"

His gaze dropped to the floor, red creeping into his cheeks. "I, ah, I've been using her as a sounding board." He smiled sheepishly. "And after I had her keep Sherry last night, I don't think she'll be surprised at all."

"I'll have to call Will, too. I don't think he'll be surprised either."

He gave her a mocking smile. "I saved your life. You belong to me now."

She put her hands on her hips. "I love you. That's why I belong *with* you."

She yelped as he tugged her to him. He wrapped his arms around her and tucked her head into his shoulder.

"That's the second time you told me you love me and the first time didn't count because we were about to make love. Shannon." His voice broke. "Your love is a gift that I'll never toss away, ever again." Tears shimmered in his eyes.

She stretched up, and kissed his cheek then his lips.

The End

Book description of **Third Choice**, Book 2 in the Choice series.

Serial Killer. Stalker. Perfect time for love?

The wife of a serial killer. That's what most people see when looking at Susan Argyle. Her life had been turned inside out six months ago, but she's recovering. Until a rabbit shows up on her doorstep with a knife through its heart. The attached note says, *You're next Murderer.* Her instant response is to call the detective with the kind eyes.

Police Detective Gary Wassman had found Susan's strength appealing when he told her that her husband had been arrested for a string of killings. Now months later, she has a stalker with murderous intent, and Gary will do anything necessary to protect her.

Can he also convince this damaged woman that she can take a chance on love again?

You can purchase this book on https://www.amazon.com

Books by Deborah Wallace

Rawlins Series (Paranormal Romance – witches)
Kathleen's Legacy
Jason's Forbidden Woman
Jamie's Trials
Adam's Redemption
Kristy's Puzzle
Tony's to Protect
Abby's Salem Legacy
Keith's Return
Gabe's Atonement

Wounded Warrior Hearts Series (Clean Romance)
Wounded Warrior Hearts: Steven
Wounded Warrior Hearts: Amy
Wounded Warrior Hearts: Russ

Choice Series (Romantic Suspense)
Second Choice
Third Choice
No Choice
Her Choice
Series Complete

Unknown Series (Romantic Suspense)
Father Unknown
Killer Unknown
Series complete

Stillwater Series (Romantic Suspense)
Returning Home

Other Books (Romantic Suspense)
I Shot the Sheriff
Your Love Belongs to Me
Summer Love
Searching for Stephanie
New Memories – Receive this book free by signing up for
    my newsletter. https://dl.bookfunnel.com/jioszdyc5a

About Deborah Wallace

Someone suggested I try writing, and stories started populating my brain, begging to be put on paper (or my computer screen).

I have been called a Jane-of-all-trades, from seamstress to house and furniture designer/builder to computer programmer to technical writer and bookkeeper. I even do car maintenance. I've also guided a team of 'Future Problem Solvers'.

I grew up in Michigan, but Massachusetts has been my home for more years than I care to think about. I love the history here, the museums and antique houses, the seacoast and hiking trails.

My three children have grown and scattered, but my husband is by my side, encouraging my writing.